The Sequel

The Sequel

A Novel

Mary Ann Peterson

ISBN: 978-1-946195-07-4

This is a work of fiction. Names, characters, places and incidents are the products of the author's imagination or are used fictitiously. Any resemblance to actual events or persons, living or dead, is entirely coincidental.

First Edition: September 2012 By North Star Press

Reprinted: February 2017

Printed in the United States of America

Reprinted by:

FuzionPrint

1250 E 115th Street

Burnsville, MN 55337

My tremendous thanks go to all the readers of *A Brief Wondrous Life* who encouraged me to write *The Sequel.*

My call to a "second journey in life" began when I found the Monticello Writer's Group. I'm grateful for our leader's critical eye and ear for making a story better.

The best advice that someone gave me was, "write the book you yourself would want to read," and that is what I have done.

Chapter One

Looking anxiously around the small cubicle as if this was a place where she didn't want to be, she drew a deep breath and sighed. There's never anything to read to relieve a person's anxiety other than the accreditations hanging on the wall. The nearest one that she was able to see read, "David L. Kantor, Gynecology, University of Chicago, Pritzker School of Medicine." The file on the small desk read "Mrs. Thomas C. Doyle," and at first that took her by surprise as she is popularly known as Jennie Rogers, her author's name. She is a New York Times bestselling author and most people have no idea what her married name is. The rain had increased to a sudden downpour, and it pounded against the roof with such force that she was momentarily distracted. Then there was a light tap on the door:

It's positive, Mrs. Doyle," Dr. Kantor announced as he entered the examining room where Jennie was nervously waiting.

"That can't be, are you sure?"

"Yes, the test results were positive."

"But I'm forty years old."

"Well, it's a little unusual at your age, but not unheard of."

"Yes, now I recall that my mother was forty years old when I was born. I didn't think I had to be careful at age 40, but I should have known better.

"You're a healthy woman; I see no reason why you won't have a perfectly normal childbirth. If you would like, in a month you could be tested to determine the sex of the fetus."

"Yes, I would like to do that."

"I think you'll actually enjoy this pregnancy. Most women aren't bothered with morning sickness in their second and third pregnancies, and they're more relaxed because of their previous experience."

Lamely, she said, "That's encouraging," and then softly murmured, "I wonder what Tom will say."

"Pardon me, I didn't hear you."

"Oh, I was just wondering what my husband will say."

Dr. Kantor smiled and said, "After an initial surprise, he will be pleased, I'm sure."

She walked through Dr. Kantor's waiting room that was now filled with pregnant women on her way to a pay phone in the hallway. She needed to talk to Suzanne, her best friend and confidant.

Their friendship began at Columbia University where they studied creative writing, and they have been close ever since.

"Hi, Suz, are you free for lunch today?"

"Yes, I am, what's up?"

"I'll tell you later. I'll swing by and pick you up in twenty minutes."

"Okay, I'll be ready."

The rain was heavier now and the thumping of the wipers, the heavy noonday traffic, and Dr. Kantor's "bombshell" made it difficult to concentrate on driving. *Do I want to raise a child at my age? Is 40 too old to be doing three a.m. feedings? Do we want to change our lifestyle? What will Tom say?* Those thoughts and others raced through her mind. Suddenly, a car pulled out in front of her, and she slammed on the brakes. Jennie stiffened with a tight grip on the steering wheel, as she subconsciously wended her way through the city and pulled up near the office door of Stein Injection Molding Company. Suzanne ran bareheaded to the car, and as she slid onto the seat, said, "So what's the big secret? Are you going to tell me you're pregnant or something?"

"Oh, Suz, you spoiled it. It was going to be a surprise. There's an Applebee's up ahead, is that okay?"

"Yes, Applebee's is fine, are you serious? I was just making a flippant remark. Are you really pregnant! I can't believe it!"

"Neither can I, I'm still in shock!

Jennie unfurled her umbrella, and they made a dash for the restaurant. After they were seated and had placed their order, Suzanne, in a serious and concerned tone of voice, asked, "Jen, how do you truly feel about this, can you handle it, do you really want another child at your age? It's a simple operation; it's not really an operation, just a simple procedure."

With her straw, Jennie stabbed at the ice cubes in her glass of water as she searched for the right words. "I thought about it on the way over, and I recalled how disappointed I was when I was carrying Charlie, and had the test and was told it was a boy. I wanted a girl, but Tom desperately wanted a boy to honor his father. I even had her name picked out. Her name would have been Peggy. I have always loved that name. If this baby would be a girl, I would be extremely happy. I'm going to take that chance."

Suzanne sighed heavily and stroked a French fry through the ketchup on her plate. "Well, this is certainly going to be a change for you and Tom. Does he know?"

"No, I didn't want to tell him over the phone. I'll tell him tonight while he is relaxing before dinner. There goes his retirement plans."

"This is awesome, Jennie, you and Tom are wonderful parents, and Charlie will like having a sister or brother. I definitely will not have another child – I still remember the pain with Lauren, but more importantly, I have become my mother's keeper, and I have a business to run. I have a full plate, and even with Matt's help, I just don't see how we could manage it."

"Yes, you do have a busy life, I can relate to that. It's just such a surprise; I wonder how Tom will react. The childbirth pain is forgotten so that doesn't bother me. I guess I've been taken by surprise and haven't accepted it yet."

"Even though I still remember Lauren's birth, she's worth every bit of pain."

"Lauren is an incredible child, and I hope this baby will be just like her."

"But there's something else I wanted to tell you. I've decided that my next book will be a sequel to "A Brief Wondrous Life."

"That's a wonderful idea. Matt will be pleased. What will the title be?

"I don't know yet. For the time being, I'm just calling it "The Sequel."

"Hey, I like that – The Sequel – it sounds mysterious; it's an attention-grabbing title."

The rain had slowed to a mist, and they slowly walked back to the car.

"Let me know how Tom reacted to the news," Suzanne said as they parted.

On the way home, she suddenly felt on the verge of tears. It had been a stressful day. The baby, and the talk she would have with Tom tonight swirled in her mind. How should she tell him? They would have to be together, just the two of them. Should they go out for a nice dinner or should she fix a nice dinner at home? She decided she would prepare dinner. Privacy and intimacy were needed.

She thought of his age, he had planned to retire. Would he feel too old to deal with another child? But Suzanne had reminded her, this is your child, too, and if you abort against your will, you will never forgive him.

While tossing the salad, Jennie rehearsed in her mind what she would say to Tom. She waited until he had mixed a drink and sat down to relax and read the paper prior to dinner before approaching him with the news.

She whiled away time in the kitchen until he had almost finished his drink so the effect of the alcohol would cushion the shock. Then she sat down next to him and completely forgetting what she had planned to say, blurted out, "I went to see Dr. Kantor today."

Tom put his newspaper down, and with an inquisitive look, said, "Don't tell me!"

"Yes, it's true, I'm almost two months pregnant. I thought we were too old for that, but as Dr. Kantor said, it does happen."

"Well, I'm a strong, virile man, and you're a beautiful, seductive woman so it's not impossible. Seriously, I think that's great," and he took Jennie's hand, pulled her close and kissed her tenderly. "Charlie needs a brother."

"No, he needs a sister!"

Chapter Two

Jennie glanced at her watch and gasped. Charlie would be waiting to be picked up from school.

She grabbed the car keys and ran out the door. While driving to the school, she thought it would be obvious there was a lack of planning having a 6th grader and a newborn. *Oh well, Charlie won't be an only child as I was and she recalled telling her parents she wished she had a sister or brother. When we were married we talked about having two children, a boy and a girl, so everything is working out as we planned. But a new baby will change everything. Well, maybe the change will be good.*

As she approached the school she could see Charlie looking around for her, and when he got into the van, as usual, she asked, "Anything exciting happen today?"

"Yes, Kevin's dog had puppies."

"I was thinking more of school, how was your day?"

"It was okay. I got a perfect score on my Social Studies test."

"That's wonderful, your father will be pleased, too."

"Mom, I'd like to have a dog. Kevin's dog had four puppies, and he has to find homes for three of them. I've always wanted to have a dog."

"Haven't you ever wanted to have a sister or a brother?"

"No, just a dog."

"Well, you're going to have a brother or a sister you know, and a new baby and a puppy might be too much to handle all at once. They both require a lot of attention."

"I'll take care of the puppy before and after school."

"In between basketball and homework? You have to discuss it with your father."

After Charlie told his father about the perfect test score, he told him about the puppy:

"Kevin's dog had puppies, and he has to find homes for three of them. They're golden labs and they're real cute. Could I have one, I've already decided to name him Sam."

"You're a little ahead of yourself. We haven't decided if we should have a dog with a new baby.

Your mother will have her hands full. Are you willing to accept responsibility for the dog?"

"Oh, yes, Dad, I'll take care of him before and after school."

"Okay, if you will help take care of it, I think we can find room for a puppy."

"Gee, thanks, Dad. You'll love him, too."

"I just might. I wanted a dog when I was your age, but mother wouldn't allow it."

"I'll call Kevin and tell him, thanks, Dad."

"You'll have to wait until the puppies have grown a bit. They say that eight weeks is the earliest a puppy should be separated from its mother."

"I know, that's what Kevin said, too. I'll help him take care of them so Sam will get to know me."

"I think that's a good idea, Charlie."

*****

Jennie had the Gender Prediction Test, and she was elated to learn that the baby was a girl. Her waistline disappeared soon after, and she readied her wardrobe for the inevitable. She stocked up on soda crackers, but so far her mornings were not consumed with bouts of nausea. Dr. Kantor told her some patients do not experience nausea at all in their second pregnancies. He told her this pregnancy might actually be enjoyable! That's doubtful! she thought.

Tom was in his mid-fifties, and although he was almost completely gray, he was still a handsome, trim and muscular man. He had planned to retire at fifty-five and devote his time to writing and public speaking. After thirty years of teaching, he wanted a change. He had always thought of joining The Speaker's Platform or a similar organization and traveling the country giving inspirational and motivational speeches. It seemed the natural step up from teaching, and he has had years of experience in inspiring his students to motivate them to excel at their subject. But now with a new baby joining the family his plans will be delayed. He also wanted to continue writing even though he already had two books published. When discussing his retirement with Jennie, he speculated: "What will be my epitaph? Writer, Professor, Legend?" Tongue in cheek, he continued, "I can see it now – A special person unforgettable for his patient tutelage of generations of Kellogg's brightest students."

Jennie had no plans to retire, and when people asked her how it felt to be a successful author, she told them, "I have to be honest and admit that nothing has changed. I still get pimples, I still have to pay my parking tickets, do the laundry and clean the bathroom just like everyone else. I go around beaming with quiet feelings of contentment for a week or so after a book is published, and then it's back to work. And the words don't come to me any easier after having four books on the shelf. I still have to work at it eight hours a day. When people ask me why I write, I tell them it's because I want to. And, that's the truth; the recognition of being a successful author is just a side note. Although I must admit that recognition is extremely gratifying."

"One day when I was in the grocery store (yes, authors do have to grocery shop) a man rushed up to me and said, "You're the lady who wrote 'A Brief Wondrous Life.' I saw you in Borders in Chicago."

"Another time, I was in Target, and a young girl ran up to me and said she had read 'The Man of Her Dreams.' She recognized me and wanted to tell me how much she enjoyed it. I treasure those moments, but I try not to let them dwell on my mind for long because they can get in the way of creativity."

"I don't try to dazzle anybody with lyricism; I write with brutal honesty and call it fiction. And, for me, it works. A Brief Wondrous Life taught me that a writer doesn't have to be brilliant to get published."

"A frequently asked question, especially by other writers, is, "Do you ever have writer's block?" I certainly do, and that's when I have my lowest self-esteem. I tell them there are times when

I'm sitting at the typewriter, ready to type, and nothing happens. Total mental block. My mind wanders back to the weekend, and I think about what happened, then I start typing and lo and behold a story unfolds. That is when I sometimes get my best ideas. I tell them they shouldn't give up. No one sits down and writes a book without working at it."

*****

Eight weeks had passed, and Charlie, Tom and Jennie were getting to know their new puppy. With his soft brown fur and pink and black nose he was adorable. Sam was a sweet little puppy who played and tumbled around like he was happy with his new home. They petted him and played with him, and he licked their faces in return. This small, laughable puppy quickly became Charlie's most loved companion, and Charlie gave back his love to Sam. All Sam asked for was unconditional love. It was evident that he was going to be one lucky dog.

Tom had bought a crate to bring Sam home, and Charlie bought him some chew toys. They had been told he was paper trained, and Tom discussed house breaking with Charlie. He also told him they needed to take him to the vet for vaccines, and he needed to be spayed. Jennie cut in and said, "The living room is off limits until he is completely housebroken." Charlie promised to take part in the training process. Since Tom got up very early to run before going to work, he volunteered to take Sam outside for his job. They started out crating him at night, and then he graduated to a dog bed in the kitchen. He had never gotten into trouble, and he had free reign of the house although he still had access to his crate if he wanted it. He loved his dog bed in the kitchen and preferred it to any other place in the house.

Sam quickly won their hearts and minds for the pure joy he brought to their lives. He didn't hide his feelings; there was no pretending that he liked his new home.

*****

Chapter Three

Mother's Day started out as a beautiful spring day, so Jennie and Tom decided to walk the three blocks to church. The service was lovely, and corsages were passed out to mothers who desired them. Jennie's back was bothering her while sitting in the straight and hard pew. She dismissed it as discomfort due to her unusually large belly. While walking home, the back pain became more intense, and Jennie tried to stand straighter to evenly distribute her weight, but the pain became stronger. As they were walking up the front walk, Jennie felt a trickle of water leave her and run down her leg. She immediately assumed her water broke, and she was going into labor. Evidently, walking to and from church brought it on.

After an hour or so, contractions started and Jennie called the doctor's answering service. The operator questioned Jennie about timing and relayed it to the doctor. She called back and told Jennie to go to the hospital.

Now the contractions were occurring two to three minutes apart. After hours of labor the pain became more and more intense as the nurses told her it was necessary for her to push the baby down into the birth canal. This went on for several hours, and Tom stayed at her side for comfort. The pain was so intense she asked for an epidural, and at that point, she would have let the night custodian administer it.

In her groggy state of mind, she barely remembered hearing the doctor say, "It's a girl!" Tom tried to awaken her to tell her Peggy Doyle was born.

*****

Charlie was upstairs in his room when Jennie and Tom brought Peggy home.

"Charlie, come down and see your little sister," Tom called from the foot of the stairs.

Charlie looked at her with an indifferent shrug, and that surprised Jennie and Tom.

"Well, what do you think of her? Isn't she cute?" Jennie asked.

"She's okay, she's just another baby," Charlie replied. "I'm going over to Kevin's to shoot some baskets."

"Don't stay long, it will soon be time for dinner," Tom replied.

"That's not what I expected. I hope he doesn't think we won't care about him now that the baby is here," Jennie said.

"No, he's just a typical 12-year old boy. At that age they are afraid to show feelings of emotion and love. They think it's a girl thing." Tom replied.

"I hope you're right."

"He'll be okay. Just give him time to get used to her being here. When he finds out she isn't competition, he'll end up protecting her with big brotherly love," Tom said.

Peggy was tucked away upstairs in the nursery which was decorated in a pink Laura Ashley circus motif. Jennie hoped she would enjoy looking at all the animals frolicking around the room. Peggy was a good baby whose only interest for now was eating and sleeping. She looked like her mother with brown hair, turned up nose and cherubic mouth. Her eyes were still blue, but they may turn to brown like her mother's. Jennie was anxious to see the bond that would develop between the two children since she was an only child. A year from now they will be more interesting to watch. She wants both Charlie and Sam to be protective of Peggy.

Suzanne and Matt couldn't wait to see Peggy, so they dropped in the same day she came home from the hospital. Suz couldn't resist taking her into her arms, and when Peggy's little bottom suddenly felt warm, she handed her off to Jennie.

While they were visiting, Matt asked Jennie about "The Sequel."

"Matt, I've put it on hold. Another idea came to mind, and I couldn't wait to get started on it."

"It must be good, what's it about?"

"It's about an elderly woman whose husband was suffering from dementia, and he remembered very little of his early years. He was 77 years old and couldn't remember what happened from age 12 on. That part of his life was a massive blur. He had been a carefree kid and then suddenly, he was a tired old man. He and his wife were married for more than 55 years, had three children, he had a great career and they had a lifetime of wonderful experiences. Now, that entire section of his life was vague and remote, almost like it didn't happen. It was like writing a message in the sand, as soon as the tide came in, it was gone. As a result, he was very despondent and depressed. To cheer him up, she began telling him fabricated stories about his life. He became so enthralled with her stories, he repeatedly asked her questions such as, "what did I do when I was twenty?" and he continued with every age that came to mind. Her stories were wonderful, warm stories about how he was a football star, a talented artist, a successful writer, etc., etc. Their lives changed completely and the deadness and despair of dementia became bearable. She loved to tell stories, and he loved to listen to them. When he passed away, she began to put her stories in writing, and she became a successful author."

"I like that, what is the title?"

"I think I'll call it, 'The Storyteller."

"Jen, that's a wonderful story, and I'm sure it would sell. I hope Peggy won't sideline your plans and inspiration."

"That won't happen immediately. She sleeps a lot now so I'll take advantage of it."

*****

One day Jennie was pacing the floor with a crying baby, and the phone rang. She hurriedly put Peggy in Charlie's arms and told him to hold her while she answered the phone. Peggy looked up at Charlie and immediately stopped crying. She stared at him with her eyes wide open as if to say, who are you, where have you been? Charlie began to laugh, and that was the beginning of a close bond that would endure for the rest of their lives.

Even though Peggy was a good baby there were moments of exasperation. She slept soundly and peacefully during the day, but at night when Tom and Jennie were exhausted and needed some sleep, she was wide awake and wanted to play. One night when they had just nodded off, Peggy's wails blasted from across the hall.

"Is she hungry?" Tom asked.

"No, she can't be hungry, go back to sleep."

"How can I? Maybe I should make sure she isn't stuck between the slats and the bumper." He went to the nursery, she was fine so he adjusted her blanket around her and the crying stopped. As he settled back in bed, the wailing resumed.

"Maybe she's wet. I'll check her diaper," and Jennie shuffled off to the nursery. Peggy was dry and warm, and she smiled. The crying stopped and Jennie gave her a kiss and returned to bed. Just as she curled up in bed, the crying started again. They pulled their blanket over their heads, but the muted sound went on.

"Whose idea was it to have this baby?"

"Not mine," she said, laughing. "Let her cry, she'll wear herself out."

The crying continued, and Tom said, "I can't sleep with that," and got out of bed.

"Don't bring her in here."

He picked her up and held her against his shoulder, lightly bouncing on his toes until his calves ached, then noticed she was sleeping. He gently laid her down, and she started to cry. He picked her up and cradled her in his arms until she appeared to be sleeping. Again, when he laid her down, she cried. "Come on, Peggy, be fair, be nice, Daddy's been up since five." He picked her up and slowly walked up and down the hallway. As long as he walked she was quiet, but if he stopped, even for a minute, she began to cry again. He continued to walk up and down the hall until he felt dizzy. Then he could feel her breath against his neck; finally she was sleeping. He gently put her back in her crib and returned to bed. "Don't say anything, let's get some sleep."

*****

Peggy grew up fast, and she was a happy child. As an energetic little three year old, a favorite game was hiding from her mother. When Jennie entered the room, she called out, "I wonder where Peggy is. I want to go outside and play, and I think Peggy would like to go, too, but I can't find her." Then Peggy would jump out from behind the sofa and say, "Here I am," and run to her mother. When Jennie caught her they would both fall down laughing. Then she hugged and kissed her. Sometimes Sam would hide with her, barking all the while, and when Jennie would stand there saying, "I can't find her," she would break down and laugh at the ridiculous scene that was being created.

She took her to the park to play on the playground equipment. They'd swing on the swings and slide down the slide and then go to the A&W where they shared a soft drink or an ice cream cone. When Peggy prattled on and on in her three-year-old speech, Jennie would put herself at Peggy's level becoming totally absorbed in her childish conversation. She imagined those afternoons, just the two of them, being happy times that Peggy would always remember.

As Peggy became more active, Sam became more protective of her. Jennie and Tom's fears of trying to raise a puppy while having a newborn baby, did not materialize and now they can't imagine their lives without Sam. He endeared himself to them in a way that they never thought possible. He was growing up to be a wonderful companion, and this house was his home every bit as much as theirs.

Charlie and Sam bonded in a special way. Charlie was his master, and he seemed to sense Charlie's every move. When it was time for Charlie to come home from school, Sam paced the floor between the front and back doors, wanting to be there to pounce on him and bark with joy. It was his way of greeting Charlie and letting him know there wasn't anyone more important in his life.

One evening when Jennie and Tom were sitting around talking, Jennie said, "I've been thinking about our vacation next year. Let's go to France, to Cote d' Azur. It's the French Riviera, the Mediterranean coastline of France. I've always wanted to go there, haven't you? We could hire a nanny to take along to stay with the kids when we wanted to get away by ourselves. Nanny jobs are very popular with college girls looking for summer employment, and vacation nannies are really in demand. "The Storyteller" would pay for the trip, and I know Matt and Suz would take Sam while we're gone."

"I, too, have always wanted to go to the Riviera, and the nanny job sounds interesting. I'm all for helping students get summer jobs. We'll keep that in mind."

A year later, Jennie and Tom had finalized their travel arrangements and tomorrow they would be boarding their Air France flight to the Riviera. Sam was ensconced at Suzanne and Matt's apartment, and Jennie hoped he wouldn't be a burden to them. Both couples couldn't bear the thought of him going to a kennel. Matt, Suzanne and Lauren had become very attached to Sam, and they were eager to enjoy his company. Lauren looked forward to taking him for walks to the park and playing with him. Jennie was having last minute jitters, but not about Sam. This was her first transatlantic flight, and before leaving she called Suz and said, "I know this is silly, but I just wanted to tell you that I love you. You know – just in case. Suz said, "I know – just in case, I love you too."

Chapter Four

Jennie lifted her sunglasses and rested them on the top of her head as she held Peggy and looked at Tom with a little frustration and some impatience. They were at the airport in Nice, France, waiting for their station wagon to take them to their Cote d'Azur resort. For some unknown reason, possibly due to language problems, they did not have a record of their reservation, so it was necessary to wait while another vehicle was being readied.

While driving to the villa they rented for two weeks, they were astonished at the beauty of the high cliffs with clustered hotels and villas impossibly built tight into them. The sea below sparkled as if it was flecked with diamonds, and the sky was a soft pale baby-blanket blue. Their villa was on a winding road near Cannes and the charming seaside resort of St. Tropez.

Sarah, their nanny who was a student at Northwestern, was equally as eager to drive up and down the Riviera coastline to explore the resort towns and sun bathe. The International Film Festival was being held in Cannes, and they hoped to see their favorite movie stars. There were museums, art gallcrics, and boutiqucs galorc in Cannes. Tom decided to hire a boat and take Charlie deep sea fishing while the girls went shopping.

While exploring Cannes, Jennie and Sarah came upon a large blue and white striped tent that was set up for an auction of art, jewelry, glassware, and anything that was worth a lot of money. Every seat was taken in the fifteen rows of white folding chairs. The only available space was in the standing room only section where onlookers were jockeying to get close enough to hear the results of the bidding. There was no apparent dress code, but most spectators were tanned and dressed to the nines.

The auctioneer keenly worked the audience; he was a consummate actor with expert timing. A painting that wasn't authenticated but "thought to be" an old master had a starting bid of $500,000. The auctioneer asked, "Do we have five-fifty?" Jennie felt a sneeze coming on, and she raised her hand to her mouth. The auctioneer looked at her and again said, "Do we have five-fifty?" Jennie shook her head and quickly ushered Peggy and Sarah from the tent. When she related the story to Tom, he laughed and said, "Always remember – don't raise your hand – sneeze if you must, but don't raise your hand."

In the evening they dressed up and went to the casino where they tried their luck and then went to trendy restaurants for a late dinner and dancing. Tom said, "I'm really glad you suggested a student nanny. She is worth her weight in gold!"

Some days they stayed at their villa and swam in their pool. Charlie and Sarah loved the pool and would have been content to live in their swimsuits. Tom bicycled to Cannes for his morning exercise and brought back food and the newspaper to keep in touch with the world. Two used bicycles came with the villa, one of which had seen better days, and the other was scruffy, but usable. Jennie teased Tom about his "Frenchness" pointing out all the old men wearing berets, and riding their bicycles with long baguettes of bread thrust in their baskets.

They made lunch at home from cheese and bread Tom bought at the bakery. They sunned beside the pool, played in the water with Charlie, Sarah and Peggy, and ate dinner late at the table next to the pool while still wearing their swimsuits. The evening air was sweet and cool. It seemed the nights were darker and the stars brighter and more numerous on the Riviera. Jennie was reminded of Van Gogh's "Starry Nights," and didn't want to leave its delightful ambience and go inside.

When they returned home and went to the Shapiro's to pick up Sam, Tom parked across the street from their apartment building. They could see Lauren outside with Sam, and when they got out of the car, Charlie shouted to Sam, and as he recognized Charlie's voice and could see him, Sam lunged forward releasing his leash from Lauren's hand and he eagerly bounded across the street to be with Charlie. Car brakes squealed, Sam let out a blood-curdling yelp of fear and pain, and then his body lay lifeless and limp in the street. Charlie ran to him and knelt down and cradled Sam's still warm little body in his arms and sobbed uncontrollably. Lauren ran to him crying and wanting to hug Sam, too. Jennie grabbed Peggy and with Tom, they ran to them and knelt in the street and cried as they held Sam's body close. All traffic stopped and several pedestrians rushed to them crying and mourning a little dog they didn't know.

It was a terrible end to a wonderful vacation, and they wondered if they would ever be able to overcome their grief and sadness. They buried Sam in an animal cemetery where they went often to visit his grave. They had Sam's likeness etched in the marble marker, and when they visited, they put fresh flowers on his grave. Sam was a member of their family, and he was treated as such.

Tom and Jennie discussed getting another dog to replace Sam, but they decided to leave that decision to Charlie. When they asked him if he would like another puppy, he told them, "I don't think any other dog could replace Sam," so they let it go at that. Tom and Jennie wondered if he was afraid he would lose another dog as he did Sam. It was hard for Charlie to let go of Sam, and Jennie thought he didn't want to go through that again. Charlie's sadness was alleviated somewhat when school got underway, and when he became busy with basketball and homework, his spirits began to lighten. He spent as much time as possible with Kevin and his dog and that seemed to help. Kevin mourned for Sam as much as Charlie did, and they consoled each other.

Matt and Suzanne grieved with them, but poor Lauren grieved the most. She felt guilty and blamed herself for the accident, but they all consoled her and tried to overcome her feelings of guilt and despair. All their friends consoled both families and told them it was okay to cry, that they had the right to grieve because they lost a loyal companion and a best friend. Soon their sadness gave way to lightheartedness and normalcy returned to their lives.

While Tom grieved, he had to prepare for another school year as his classes at the Kellogg School of Business resumed the following week, and he found it difficult to concentrate on his studies. Sam's death was as traumatic for him as it was for Charlie. He had become attached to Sam as they went for their early morning walks. Sam was not just a dog, he was like a pal and trusted companion. He became the childhood pet Tom never had.

*****

At sixteen, Charlie was tall with a thick head of brown hair and penetrating dark eyes. He had many friends, and their voices and laughter echoed around the house. He pretended he wasn't interested in girls, but there were certain girls he noticed, and he did not go unnoticed by them. Basketball was the only organized sport he ever played, and that was only in Middle School. He preferred to spend hours by himself reading, but he and Kevin shot baskets in the driveway whenever they were together. When the weather was nice, as soon as he got home from work and had changed out of his suit, Tom joined them in the driveway for scuttle. Even when the weather wasn't nice, there were plenty of times they'd be out there dribbling and shooting.

Now that Charlie had his learner's permit and was driving, he wanted to have extra money for gas, so he found a summer job at Wrigley Field. Tom wanted him to learn the responsibilities of driving by contributing toward gasoline. He didn't want Charlie to think he could drive and drive around and bring the car home with an empty tank.

He also had a car fund and tried to save money for his own car. One day he told Tom, "I already have three hundred and thirty four dollars. By next summer I should have enough for a good used car." In the winter he shoveled snow and did other odd jobs to earn money, but he had to keep up with his studies, too. "School comes first," Tom told him.

Lauren was fifteen and was active in soccer. Jennie and Tom often shared a blanket with Suzanne and Matt at her games. Jennie and Suz enjoyed seeing Lauren grow from adolescence into the world of teenagers, and when they overheard her conversations with friends they were reminded of their own candid discussions at the coffeehouse after their creative writing classes.

She inherited her mother's best features, and she was a beautiful girl. She had her mother's olive skin, which stayed tan from early spring through December, and her green eyes. She was a combination of her mother's and her father's good looks. But Lauren had no idea how lovely or how lucky she was.

Lauren attended Hebrew school, and when she was thirteen, she had her bat mitzvah. The ceremony took place at 10 a.m. at Temple Sholom where Suzanne and Matt were married. After the ceremony, they all went to the Drake for a luncheon and dancing to the music of a DJ.

Lauren was beautiful in a black dress with short puffy sleeves, fitted bodice and short flared skirt. Her shiny brown hair was cut to the perfect length for the shape of her face, and she was exquisite. Peter, her boyfriend, was wearing a turquoise polyester tux that was trimmed in black, possibly to match the aquamarine tablecloths with seashell centerpieces on the tables in the dining room.

When Tom and Jennie entered the dining room, Suz swept them to a table saying, "You are sitting with us." They also shared the table with Rabbi Goldman and his wife, Alice, and Matt's parents, Sidney and Ethel Shapiro, who came from New York City for the event. The Goldman's had moved from New York City a year ago, so they had much in common. Lauren and Peter were seated at a separate table with their friends.

The dance floor was topped with glittering disco balls, and they watched as Peter led Lauren to the dance floor for the first dance to music that blared so loudly the silverware shivered with fear. Suzanne kept a close eye on Lauren as they had heard that some bar and bat mitzvah's were starting to get out of hand. "Suz, I don't think you have to worry about Lauren, she has a good head on her shoulders, and you and Matt have been involved parents, always being there for her," Jennie remarked.

When a child reached thirteen, the age of Jewish adulthood, and became a bar or bat mitzvah, they were encouraged to do deeds of charity and extend loving kindness in the world. Lauren took that seriously; after college she was determined to join the Peace Corps. She wanted to do her share to make the world a better and healthier place. Suzanne and Matt wanted her to go East to school, but she wanted to go to Northwestern because her friends were going there. She had her life all planned. After college and the Peace Corps, she would work at Stein Injection Molding, stating that she would one day become the CEO. She wanted to carry on the tradition of the eldest or only son taking control of the family business. She remembered taking walks with her grandfather. He grasped her hand in his left hand as he hobbled along stooped and clutching his cane with his right hand. He was not one for reciting children's stories, so he made up stories about little plastic parts and the equipment used to make them. At her tender age, she thought the stories were as exciting as "The Three Bears." Suzanne was proud that Lauren wanted to follow in her footsteps.

Peggy was in second grade at Frances W. Parker, a private school, so each morning Amy and Jennie dropped her off at 8 a.m. and picked her up in the afternoon. Amy was Peggy's Barbie doll, and she went wherever Peggy went. When Peggy came along Tom saw the need for a larger car, so they had traded the Grand Prix for the Volvo. It has taken them on several vacations and it was now idling in the after school pick-up line of cars at Peggy's school. It has and will continue to see its share of boisterous boys and giggling girls.

Peggy liked school; she liked to listen to Miss Ella read stories to the class. Jennie also read to her at night before she went to bed. Tom and Jennie were avid readers, and they hoped she would become a reader as well.

*****

Chapter Five

Tom and Jennie still liked to jog and run, and one Saturday after a usual long run they sat at the kitchen table talking and slowly sharing a cup of coffee. Tom quickly put his hand to his chest and winced. Jennie abruptly changed the subject and asked, "What's wrong, Tom?"

"Just a little pain in my chest. It was nothing."

"Chest pain? You are having chest pains?" She asked again remembering that both their fathers died young from heart attacks.

Tom reluctantly admitted he had a stabbing pain, but it slowly subsided. "It was nothing – it's gone now."

Nevertheless, Jennie insisted that he see a cardiologist and have a stress test. She checked and was given the name of a prominent cardiologist in Chicago, and then made the appointment for him. Even though Tom was reluctant, he saw the doctor and was given a stress test. The doctor told Tom that his stabbing pain was angina pains, and he should have an angiogram. He had his nurse make an appointment at the hospital, and the appointment was scheduled for a week later.

The doctor advised Tom what he needed to do prior to the test, i.e., fasting and medications to avoid prior to testing. The nurse told him when to arrive at the hospital and where to go.

Jennie suggested that he ease up on his running until after the test, but Tom persisted, saying there was nothing to worry about, he felt fine, and it was simply a routine test. Jennie tried to be as unconcerned as Tom, but she knew there had to be a serious reason for the angiogram. She tried to concentrate on her writing, but her mind wandered and went blank.

Saturday finally arrived, and Jennie accompanied Tom to the hospital. He was taken to the Cath Lab, and she waited for what seemed an interminable long time. Finally, the doctor came and asked her to come into his office. After she was seated, he told her, "We are going to admit your husband. He has blockage in the left coronary artery, and we need to do an angioplasty procedure and put two stents in the artery to keep it open. It is a fairly routine procedure, but because of his age, we want to keep him another day and monitor his progress."

Jennie was relieved that Tom had the test, and she was grateful that the doctor used precaution and did the angioplasty.

"What was the cause of the blockage," she asked.

"It's a build-up of plaque caused from high cholesterol; it's a very common malady. Many people have a problem with high cholesterol and take medication to try to bring it down. We'll have to put Tom on medication, too. As soon as your husband is admitted, he will be assigned a room. Then we'll proceed with the angioplasty and take him to his room afterward. Then you'll be able to visit with him."

"How long will the angioplasty take and how long will it be before he is taken to his room?"

"The angioplasty doesn't take long. You should be able to see him in about two hours. You can wait in the lounge next to the Cath Lab, then you'll see him when he comes out. In the meantime, the nurse will let you know his room number, and you could wait for him there, if you like."

When Tom was wheeled from the lab, Jennie went to him and asked how he was. He stated, "It was a breeze, in fact; I watched the whole procedure on closed circuit TV. I feel fine."

After visiting for a few minutes, Jennie left as Tom had to lie absolutely still for a few hours, and the nurses were doing blood work and hooking him up to IV's. When she returned in the morning, Tom had just finished his breakfast, and the nurse told him the doctor would see him momentarily.

When the doctor arrived, he discussed with Tom what he needed to do in the next few weeks. He shouldn't drive for a few days, take the medication that was prescribed to prevent clotting, change his bandage, do not lift anything heavier than 5 pounds, and only do the daily exercises that were prescribed.

The doctor also recommended that in a month from now he should go through the cardiac rehabilitation program at the hospital, and he gave him the phone number to call to get on their schedule.

After arriving home, they sat down at the kitchen table and went through his prescriptions, schedules of exercise, and do's and don'ts. It would be a new way of life for him. He had always prided himself for being healthy and free of medical problems.

He called the number of Cardiac Rehab to make an appointment.

"What should I bring?" He asked.

"Sneakers, shorts, and a T-shirt."

"No seriously!"

"I am serious. You'll be on the tread mill, exercise bike, rowing machine and other equipment. We want to get your blood flowing and give your heart a good workout. The human heart is just a pump, but it's an incredibly important pump, and we need to know that its performing properly. Of course, you'll be monitored throughout the exercise regime."

Jennie commented, "I'm disgustingly healthy except for a touch of arthritis and you have inherited

Chapter Six

On a slushy, gray February afternoon, Jennie stopped at Whole Foods on her way to pick up Peggy, and she thought as she drove up that it was only yesterday that their windows twinkled with tiny white Christmas lights. Now they were emblazoned with hopeful red and pink hearts, and that reminded her of Valentine's Day at Parker school. They sold sugar cookies shaped like hearts with pink and red frosting, and little cards were attached for a message. The students bought them for their friends at school and sold them to their families and friends away from school. It was a popular fund raiser. Each cookie cost a dollar, and all the money went to the school's building fund. The students tried to outdo each other to see who could sell the most cookies. Tom was usually their best customer buying them from Peggy so she had a chance at being a top salesperson. Jennie thought to herself, *It will be interesting to see how many he buys this year. He won't want to disappoint Peggy and he won't want to have them around as temptation. It will be a dilemma to deal with.*

The subject came up at the dinner table, and Tom told Peggy he would buy cookies from her to pass out to his students. Jennie smiled approvingly.

Peggy was elated; she would have a chance to be the top producer this year.

On Valentine's Day, Peggy came home from school thrilled and excited. She received a Valentine cookie from a boy named Steve Brosky, and her comment was, "I barely know who he is, why would he give me a cookie?"

Tom volunteered, "Maybe he bought a cookie for everyone in class so he would win the top producer's award."

Peggy suddenly looked downcast, and Tom realized his remark hurt her feelings. So he told her, "I think Steve gave you the cookie because you're the cutest girl in class."

Her face lit up, and she smiled with the secure thought in her mind that Steve Brosky liked her.

Jennie thought, *she's way too young to be thinking about boys,* and she was reminded of a recent conversation when someone asked her about Peggy's age, and she replied, "She's seven." "Seven, he said scornfully, "Soon she'll be twenty." "Yikes, he was right!"

Later, Jennie remarked to Tom, "I wonder who Steve Brosky is and what he looks like."

"He probably wears glasses as thick as Coke bottles, or else he's the type who wears his hair in dreadlocks."

The following day Jennie had a surprise when she picked up Peggy at school. Peggy emerged from the school with a boy who resembled a miniature football player. He was small and muscular, a feisty little guy, who wore his hair in a short crew cut. They were both laughing, and when Peggy climbed in the Volvo, she said, "That's Steve."

"Oh, he's cute," Jennie murmured, and her remark went unanswered.

When she related the incident to Tom, he said, "Maybe we'll have a star quarterback in the family."

"Let's let her grow up, I'm not ready to hand her over to someone else."

*****

When Charlie turned seventeen he had his driving license and was shopping for a used car. He had been doing odd jobs for Mrs. Dillard, who lived a few blocks away, and he noticed that her old ’72 Gremlin sat in the garage unused most of the time. He spent hours inspecting every inch of the car, running his hand over the racing stripes, wondering why an old lady would have a car with racing stripes.

“That was my son’s car, he gave it to me when he bought a new one. But because of my bad eyes, I can’t drive any more.”

“I’ve been saving money for a car.”

“I’d like to sell it while it’s still in good condition. If you ‘re interested, you can have it for $500.00.”

“I have to have my father’s approval.”

“Yes, your daddy should help you buy your first car.”

He told his father all about the car, and they took it out for a drive. Tom said it was a good car for the price, it had low mileage, tires were good, it drove well, and the interior was spotless. So Charlie became the owner of a butterscotch-gold Gremlin with racing stripes.

Charlie circled the Gremlin letting his fingers brush against the cool metal in a gesture of admiration as if he had built it himself. He kicked the tires, and inspected its finish, telling his father he would wash and polish it often. He would never drive a dirty car, the car deserved more respect that that.

"I think you got a good deal, son, this car is in A-1 condition. Maybe you should take your mother for a ride."

He went in the house and called for Jennie. "Hey, Mom, would you like a ride in my new car?"

"Yes, I would. I was just going to go to the grocery store, so I'll let you drive me."

"Oh, this is nice," as she settled in the front seat. "Mrs. Dillard evidently didn't drive much, the upholstery is like new. I wonder why she sold it."

"Her eyesight is real bad, and she has bad arthritis in one leg. She limps, says it's very painful."

"Well, that's a shame. I'm glad you help her out."

"Yeah, I like working for her. She's real nice, says I remind her of her son when he was young, and she always serves cookies and Kool-Aid or Lemonade when I finish my work."

"She's very thoughtful. Whole Foods is in the next block."

He pulled up to the store to let her out.

"Why don't you park and come inside and help me."

Charlie was planning to wait in the car and try out the radio, but he reluctantly parked and went inside. He followed his mother up and down the aisles steering the cart. A number of women greeted her, and she introduced each of them to Charlie, saying, "I want you to meet my son, Charlie. Charlie, this is Mrs. Wilson, and it went on and on. All the women fawned over him, and he felt awkward and tried to hurry his mother, but she was proud of him and wanted everyone to know he was her son. He began to regret offering her a ride. And if that wasn't enough, the shopping cart had a squeaky wheel that spun in the opposite direction from the other three. He constantly had to maneuver it to go straight.

Finally, they were in the checkout lane, but the introductions continued. He sighed with relief as he loaded the bags in the trunk. She thanked him when the last bag was brought in and put on the kitchen counter.

"Mom, I'm going to drive over to Kevin's now, I'll be home shortly."

His arm hung out the window as he and Kevin drove up and down the street waving to passing children remembering what it was like to be young and innocent, and he thought to himself *someday you'll be driving your first car up and down this same street.* Charlie and Kevin's friendship deepened after Sam was killed. They mourned and grieved together, and the bond between them was strengthened. They became inseparable friends, and they enjoyed riding in the car together.

The two boys were most often seen wearing dirty white T-shirts while washing and waxing the car to a lustrous shine. They used old cloth diapers and applied three coats of wax, buffing between each coat, and then they stood back to admire the sheen. They installed a new air filter, tested the air pressure in the tires, and spent hours working under the hood or rolling back and forth under the car while Peggy went to and from the house keeping them supplied with glasses of Kool-Aid.

Charlie still worked at Wrigley Field in the summer and now he could drive to and from work instead of taking the bus.

Charlie and Kevin enrolled in their first year of college at Northwestern, and they drove to and from Evanston each day. Charlie didn't want to live on campus because he wouldn't be able to have a car. The two boys were good students, and now that they were in college they spent hours talking about their studies and their futures. Kevin was passionate about becoming a veterinarian, and Charlie wanted to follow in his father's footsteps and be a college professor. He majored in history and social studies, and he wanted to teach at Columbia University in New York City.

*****

Tom and Jennie got the call at 1:10 in the morning. The man said, "Unresponsive driver '72 Gremlin totaled. He's being taken to Northwestern. The other boy has lacerations, but will be okay."

Tom was stunned by what he was hearing in his groggy, half-awake state, and he blurted out to Jennie, "Charlie's been in an accident. Hurry and get dressed," as he put his shirt and pants on over his pajamas. Jennie grabbed her slacks and sweater and dressed as quickly as possible.

As they were driving to the hospital, Jennie asked if Charlie crashed into another car. "The radio dispatcher didn't mention another vehicle, but he must have crashed into something," Tom replied.

"What about Kevin?"

"He said the other boy has lacerations and will be okay." He pulled into the ER parking lot, and they ran to the triage door.

"We're here for Charlie Doyle, how is he?" Tom asked the nurse at the desk.

"He's still non-responsive, but they're working on him. He doesn't have head injuries," she said and looked at Jennie as if she was reading her mind.

"Oh, that's a relief," Jennie replied. "How is the other boy?"

"He has some facial lacerations, and they're checking him for internal injuries. He's banged up, but he'll be okay. You can sit in the waiting room, and we'll let you know when things change."

The police officer who was called to the scene of the accident came up to the desk to get information on the victims to complete his report. Tom went over to him and asked what happened. He asked Tom if he was the father, then handed him a speeding ticket saying the car was clocked at 70 MPH on a city street – Ridge Avenue – lost control, smashed into a tree. No alcohol. He'll have to go to court, he continued, and handed Tom the car keys.

Tom sighed as the words raced through his mind – speeding, unconscious, court. This was his son, Charlie, who had never been in trouble. He thanked the officer and told him he would handle everything.

As he finished talking to the officer, Kevin's parents rushed in and came over to talk to Tom and Jennie. They had received word that Kevin would be momentarily released, but Charlie was still unconscious, and they consoled Tom and Jennie. Then there was a call from the desk for Mr. and Mrs. Doyle. They were told that Charlie had regained consciousness, and they were checking him thoroughly for internal injuries. If nothing was found he would be released.

When Charlie was released and saw his parents, he knew he was in trouble. Tom put his arm around Charlie's shoulder and asked how he was. Charlie said he had the worst headache of his life and every bone in his body was sore.

"Can I just go home and go to bed, Dad?'

Tom told him that would be okay; they would have their talk later.

Charlie knew he was in trouble, and he wouldn't get out of it unless he admitted guilt. "I did a stupid thing, Dad, and I'm sorry you have to be involved. I accept complete responsibility for this mess."

"It may not be that simple, son. You'll have to go to court. The worst scenario would be losing your driver's license. The easy way out of this mess would be a fine. It will probably be a steep fine; fines are based on every mile over the speed limit. Thank God you weren't drinking. Alcohol increases a fine considerably."

"I'll admit I'm guilty, be polite, and tell them that next week I have to leave for a teaching position at Columbia. Hopefully, everything can be taken care of before I have to leave."

"Charlie, I hope it will be that simple."

Charlie inspected the wrecked Gremlin that had been towed away. Tears glistened in his eyes, and he didn't care who saw him.

The following Monday Charlie had to appear in traffic court in downtown Chicago. Tom drove and this was Charlie's first visit to the Daley Center. He checked in with the clerk and was directed to a sitting area where he was told to wait to be called. The courtroom reeked of a mixture of sweat and cigarette smoke, and he was in awe as he watched the assortment of inner-city offenders who appeared before the judge. He was seated next to a heavy-set man whose face appeared puffed with rage and ready to explode. He was sitting so close beside him that he could almost feel his sweaty skin next to his own skin. The man asked him, "Wwha'd they git you for?"

Charlie replied, "Speeding, and you?"

DUI was his blunt reply.

Charlie didn't want to continue the conversation so he turned to his father who also was taken aback by the characters and goings-on in the courtroom. They were stunned to hear the profanity-laced dialogue of those who appeared before the judge.

The wait was long, but for Charlie the scenario that was being played out in the courtroom was riveting. He stood out from the others in the room because he was clean shaven, his hair was clean and combed, and his shirt and pants were clean and pressed.

When he was finally called to the stand, he politely addressed the judge and replied "guilty, your honor" when asked, and he spoke with humility. He was placed on unsupervised probation on condition he pay a fine of $100.00 and $48.00 in court costs for driving 70 mph in a posted 45 mph zone. It was a new experience for Charlie, and one that he did not wish to repeat.

The following week he was flying off to New York City, shooting down the runway at O'Hare in a big, gleaming jet, his eyes moist from the sadness of leaving Lincoln Park and Chicago where he was born and would only see again on holidays. His father would jokingly call him "the frequent flyer."

He had accepted a position at Columbia University teaching graduate students United States history and social studies, and he had barely completed his own doctorate. If his future seemed daunting, it didn't show. His new home was the faculty housing project: dark red brick row houses with white shutters, and gleaming black iron railing along the stoop, near the campus in Morningstar Heights, and he would share office space with others in the history department at Fayerweather Hall. He needed to fend for himself now. He would be building his future from the ground up.

*****

Years later when Jennie was at her desk and inspiration had eluded her she thought back to the day Dr. Kantor told her she was pregnant and she might have the daughter she had longed for. *One of the things I hadn't anticipated was how entertaining it would be. My darling daughter, Peggy, and I spend hours together, and I've gotten to know her every expression, the lilt of her voice, her anxiety and enthusiasm. Her current interests include Girl Scouts, slumber parties, soccer and riding her bicycle with friends. She is very good at soccer and is the goalie on her team. She also is a good student. I am constantly amazed at how savvy she is, how much more pop-culturally aware she is than I was at her age.*

Peggy surprised Jennie and Tom when she announced that she wanted to see the movie, "Dirty Dancing."

They told her she couldn't see it until she was in high school because it was rated R.

"But, Dad, it's just a movie."

"I'm glad you are mature enough to realize that, but it contains suggestive scenes and offensive language that your mother and I feel are for more adult minds. Let's wait a year, and if you still want to see it, then it will be okay."

They also had varying opinions when it came time to shop for her high school prom dress. The pink or blue dresses would not do at all; she gravitated toward the skinny black floor-length gowns. She had been waiting forever for her prom, limos and all-night parties. If it had been just another dance she'd have bought the dorky blue dress her parents liked. But this was *the prom.* It was supposed to be different.

When they forbid her to get a black gown she opted for a silvery pink number with spaghetti straps that made her look 30 years old. She piled her hair on top of her head and put on a pair of heels. When her parents told her they didn't think it was appropriate for the occasion, she said, "What do you think is going to happen to me if I wear it? Do you think that just because I'm showing my shoulders I'd have sex or something?"

They continued shopping, and at Lord & Taylor the saleslady found the perfect dress for her. When Peggy first saw it, she said it wasn't what she was looking for, but after trying it on she fell in love with it and so did her mother. The dress was made of dark green taffeta, it was sleeveless with a low neckline and form-fitting bodice, and the full skirt fell gracefully to her ankles. Jennie suggested that she have white satin pumps dyed to match the dress, and they found the perfect gold necklace that complimented the dress perfectly. Her father told her she looked like a princess. Like the black dress, the limo and all-night parties existed only in her imagination.

One afternoon Jennie had curled Peggy's hair with the curling iron and was brushing it out when Peggy casually said, "You know, Mom, I've done it."

Jennie's hand abruptly stopped in its path, and she quietly said, "Are we talking about what I think we're talking about?"

"Are you mad?"

Jennie shook her head, dazed. "When?"

"Last year."

Jennie was stunned. It happened a year ago and she didn't know. "Who?"

"Remember Jason?"

"You were only fourteen!" Jennie said disbelieving what she was hearing.

"Why?" Jennie asked suddenly realizing it was a ridiculous question.

"I just wanted to try it, other girls do it," Peggy answered.

"Once?" Jennie asked.

Peggy nodded.

"Did you like it?" Jennie asked.

"No, it hurt. I told Jason I didn't want to do it again. He said he didn't either, so we stopped seeing each other."

Jennie hugged her and said, "I'm glad you told me."

"I wanted to before, but I thought you'd be mad and you'd probably have to tell Daddy."

"Well, I'm not mad at you, but I want you to know it's an important part of life. It's something special, and it does mean something. You need to wait until you've met the right boy. Your father would tell you the same thing."

"I know that now."

Chapter Seven

The only sound was an airplane passing overhead. It had begun its descent in preparation for landing at O'Hare. Through the window, Jennie watched it imagining the people aboard straining in their seats looking down at where they would soon be arriving. Jennie was sitting by the kitchen window drinking coffee and adding some last minute items to the list of groceries she would shortly go shopping for their Thanksgiving dinner.

The phone rang, and Charlie's voice said, "Hi, Mom, we'll be landing shortly. I finished my classes and was able to get an earlier flight. Can you pick me up at the airport?"

Before he could finish his conversation, there was an enormous noise that sounded like an explosion, then a gigantic crashing sound, and then an eerie silence. She grabbed the car keys and ran out the door.

Tom had gone to the University of Illinois in Champaign to pick up Peggy, and she glanced at her watch thinking they would soon be on their way home. It was a four-hour drive to Chicago, and as she turned her radio on, she wondered if he would have his car radio tuned to the news station and hear about the accident.

When she turned onto the exit leading to the airport terminal, police cars were everywhere stopping cars and directing them away from the terminal except for a couple of cars that were allowed through. She told the officer that her son was on a flight arriving from New York, and she told him about Charlie's conversation and the loud crashing noise. He directed her in the same direction as the other two cars saying that relatives of passengers were being allowed to go to a holding area to await the outcome of the accident.

The voice on the radio was almost drowned out from the noise of sirens and static, but it appeared that one of the 747's engines exploded as the plane touched down on the runway, and then the plane's nose crashed into the barrier fence at the end of the runway before it was brought to a standstill. The fate of the passengers was as yet unknown.

When Jennie arrived at the holding area, the people assembled there were intermittently crying and talking as they waited for their loved ones to enter the room. They spoke of them as if they had been injured and may or may not survive. Jennie distanced herself and anxiously waited hoping to hear an update on when the passengers would be released when a security guard opened a door and told the crowd to stand back and let the passengers walk freely into the holding area. She eagerly scanned each face and then saw Charlie at the end of the line. At the same time he saw her, he waved and smiled. When they were united, she cried and hugged him, asking over and over, "How are you?"

"Mom, I'm okay, but there are others who were badly shaken and possibly injured. It was awful."

"Well, I'm so glad that you are okay, and I hope everyone else will be okay."

As Tom was driving back to Chicago he heard all about the crash on the car radio and assumed it was Charlie's flight. Hearing that most of the passengers were safe and uninjured, he thought to himself, *Thank God – I can't wait to get home and see him.*

When they all were at home and Charlie was telling them about the crash, he said, "I was sitting in the middle of the cabin and all hell broke loose when the engine exploded. We all thought we were goners. It's a miracle the plane didn't catch on fire. Then almost immediately paramedics entered the plane and were taking the injured to a line of waiting ambulances. Everything was happening so fast we were amazed at the rescue operations."

As they watched the TV coverage, the newscaster said the crew's last communication indicated the plane was on a normal landing approach with no mention of any problems. They think a bird may have caused the explosion, but that's always the first thing that comes to mind.

Continuing, he said all passengers survived and only two were hospitalized. They said rescue crews reached the plane within minutes after the explosion.

Tom put his arm around Charlie's shoulders and said, "That was close, son, we have a lot to be thankful for this Thanksgiving."

When Jennie came home from shopping, she put the celery and onions aside and began dicing them for the dressing. Then she thought of Charlie's ordeal and of him being so far away. It was his first year of teaching at Columbia University in

New York, and they would be lucky to share holidays with him.

In the evening it began to snow – tiny flakes that made it look like the ground was being salted. In the morning when they looked out the window, they were almost blinded from the brightness. It had snowed all night and the ground was covered. They had made plans to go jogging and then have breakfast at the pancake house a few blocks away. The smell of bacon greeted them as they entered, and they immediately ordered large steaming cups of coffee. The snow was an early surprise, and with the sun streaming in the windows, Tom assured Charlie and Peggy it would be gone by afternoon.

When they returned home, Tom put the turkey that he had prepared earlier in the oven. They all planned to have a relaxing day at home, and Peggy emerged from her room dressed in slim black pants and a black cashmere turtleneck sweater, her long hair piled on top of her head and held in place with a huge silver barrette. Gone was the innocent, round-cheeked, plump little girl with long bangs covering her forehead. Now, she was coltishly slender in a very feminine way. A true brunette, she was blessed with richly textured hair that fell over her shoulders. She reminded Jennie of her and Suzanne when they were students at Columbia in Chicago, and she recalled their after-class meetings at the coffee house dressed in slim jeans and a black turtleneck, their long hair tucked behind their ears in the fashion of the day. Tom commented, "Our pretty little girl is growing up to be a beautiful young woman."

A partially-completed jigsaw puzzle was spread out on a table, and they all tried to put the pieces together while the turkey was roasting in the oven.

Finally, they all assumed their assigned place in the kitchen, and in no time they were sitting around the table.

"As I have said before," Jennie told Tom, "You are the better cook. This turkey is perfect."

"That's not true," he said, but he was pleased. "The dressing is truly delicious."

After they had eaten their last bite of turkey, Charlie and Peggy began clearing the table in anticipation of dessert – a choice of apple pie with ice cream or pumpkin pie with whipped cream. Tom poured coffee.

As they were eating, they admired the mural on the dining room wall and recalled the renovation that seemed so long ago. Jennie reminisced about the many dinner parties they have enjoyed in this room which is her favorite. Peggy said the beautiful mural depicting an ocean scene was her favorite part of the house, saying that it gave her the feeling that she wanted to stay and linger at the table. She told her parents that she was studying interior design, because she liked to create beautiful surroundings. Jennie commented, "I think you have made a good decision."

Sooner than expected, it was time to get ready for Christmas. The usual cookies and other treats came first – they could be frozen and out of the way as shopping and entertaining took center stage. Even though Charlie and Peggy wanted to be with their friends, Jennie and Tom wanted to share them with their friends, too. They stayed home to greet and meet their friends at their annual open house party, and then they went off to mingle with their own friends. They had grown up to be gracious and polite hosts, and Tom and Jennie were very proud of them. When Christmas had been celebrated, it was sad to have Charlie return to New York, and Peggy to the University of Illinois in Champaign where she was in her freshman year studying architecture and interior design.

Chapter Eight

One of the pleasures of being a parent are the surprises that crop up when you least expect them. Peggy called on Thursday to tell them she was coming home for the weekend. She was in her sophomore year at the University of Illinois, and she didn't own a car. She told them she would be getting a ride with Steve Brosky, and Jennie's memory was jolted back to the Valentine cookie fundraiser at Francis W. Parker School in Lincoln Park. That was the last time his name was mentioned, and now more than ten years later Peggy calmly mentioned she would be riding home with him from college. They didn't even know he was attending the same school. Now that she has grown up, the thought occurred that maybe she was bringing a boyfriend home for her parent's approval.

When Jennie told Tom about the call, it was also his first impression. "I didn't expect to ever hear about Steve Brosky again."

"I didn't either; this is going to be an interesting weekend.

Friday evening Peggy bounced into the house and cheerfully called out "Hi, Mom, Hi, Dad." After the usual hugs and kisses, she went to the kitchen and opened the refrigerator looking for something to eat.

"What do you have for a sandwich, I'm starved."

How about a peanut butter sandwich," Tom replied as he grabbed a loaf of bread.

"That's fine." She ripped off the tab on the top of a soda can and sat down at the kitchen table.

They all started talking at once and then Jennie finally asked about Steve Brosky. "How did you and Steve get together?"

"He's also studying to be an architect so we share some classes. That's how we met. When I first saw him, he greeted me by name, and that surprised me because I didn't recognize him. I didn't think he would know me after all these years."

"I knew you the first day you came to class, he said. After that, we started dating."

"Do you see each other often?"

"Not as often as we would like. He's on the football team, so he doesn't have much spare time."

"Oh, what position does he play?" Tom asked.

"He's a quarterback."

"What do you know about him, what does his father do?"

"He's in the construction business, they build everything from houses to commercial buildings."

"What is Steve's nationality? Have you ever talked about that?" Jennie volunteered.

"Yes, he mentioned that his father was Russian, and his mother was Polish. His grandparents fled Poland when the Nazis occupied the country. They came to America with only a change of clothing in one suitcase. He's real proud of his family."

Tom asked her again about Steve's football experience. "You said he's a good quarterback, does he ever hope to play professional ball?"

"No, he wants to go into business with his father."

Jennie glanced at the clock and said, "It's getting late, we should be turning in. We can talk more tomorrow."

Over breakfast, Steve's name came up again. Jennie had asked Peggy if she dated anyone other than Steve.

"No, I haven't because I haven't met anyone I would consider dating. Maybe it'll be different next semester."

"I hope you will get to know other boys and not get serious about Steve," Jennie replied.

"Mother, we aren't serious, we just have fun together. And, I don't have a lot of time for dating. My courses require a lot of homework, and Steve has less free time. He's either doing homework or practicing football."

"I'm happy to hear you are keeping up with your studies," Jennie said, and she thought to herself: *My beautiful daughter is smarter than I give her credit for. She knows what she wants, and she's going after it..*

"What are you studying now? Are you into home designs?"

"Not yet. Right now we're into arches. Do you know how many different kinds of arches there are? There are flat arches, round arches, triangular arches, pointed arches, so many arches I've never heard of."

Jennie laughed, "I don't think we need to know what they are."

"Incidentally, we will be going to the 9 o'clock service at church, would you please go with us?" Peggy said she would, saying, "I don't go to church every Sunday, but Steve does – he's Catholic."

Jennie's thoughts went back to Steve Hollis, her first love. Why does his name have to be Steve? It was painful to recall that part of her life; she had thought it was buried back in time. She reminded herself that they weren't serious, and she feigned interest saying, "That's nice."

"What's going on for Christmas this year?" Peggy asked.

"Oh, I'm glad you asked, I might have forgotten. Charlie's bringing his girlfriend.

"Really! Good ole conservative Charlie has a girlfriend! Is she a teacher?"

"That was my first thought, but he said she's in the computer business. At least, we know she's smart."

"Not necessarily, but she evidently has a good memory. You have to memorize all the functions of a computer. Mom, you should have a computer for your writing. It would save you so much work. And, get a printer, too."

"Yes, a printer would save me all those trips to Kinkos."

Tom had been listening, and he smiled in agreement. "I think that's a good idea." Now he knew what he would get Jennie for Christmas.

Jennie continued saying, "We'll do the usual, go to church, open gifts Christmas Eve, and have a big dinner on Christmas day. Why don't you invite Steve for Christmas dinner? It would be interesting and fun to have the four of you here."

"That would be fun. I'll do that."

Sunday was a beautiful, sunny fall day, and the crimson and gold leaves on the sidewalk crunched as they walked the three blocks to church. After a lunch of cold chicken, potato salad, and orange slices, the doorbell rang as Steve arrived on time to pick up Peggy.

He was as good looking as she was beautiful with windblown, thick brown hair and dark brown eyes that sported the longest lashes ever seen on a man. He looked like an overgrown boy. He had wide shoulders, but he was slim in the hips. He had a lazy grin that immediately brought a smile to Jennie and Tom's faces. *The cute little boy at Peggy's grade school has grown up to be a handsome college boy.* There was gentleness in his voice as he said, "Good afternoon,

Mr. and Mrs. Doyle, I'm Steve Brosky, and I've come to take your daughter back to school." He extended his hand, and Tom eagerly took his hand in his.

"We're so glad you brought her with you. We miss her terribly, and we were happy to have her home for the weekend," Jennie replied.

Peggy had stepped forward with her backpack and was ready to leave. "Thanks, Mom and Dad," and she hugged both of them good bye.

"Good bye, darling, it was good to have you with us.

"What a nice young man," Jennie remarked as she closed the door.

"Yes, he seems to be very nice. I think our little girl is in good company."

*****

Now that Charlie and Peggy were away at school or occupied with their own friends, they weren't always at home for every holiday. Tom and Jennie were faced with their absence on Thanksgiving, so the invitation to have dinner and reconnect with her childhood friends, Lynn and Roger Smith in Quincy, was enthusiastically received. Their trips to Quincy had become less and less frequent over the years, and Lynn and Roger didn't have children to share their holidays so they were eager to see Jennie and Tom.

Jennie offered to bring the oyster dressing that she and Tom had perfected, and Lynn graciously accepted saying, "Dressing is one thing I just can't get right, but I think you'll like Roger's bourbon-glazed sweet potatoes. He got the recipe from a cooking show on TV. He tries all their recipes. He even threw out all our old pots and pans and bought shiny red ones from Pampered Chef. He will probably give you a tour of our new kitchen and show them off to you."

"Well, I certainly hope so, Tom and I are always interested in the latest cookware."

Traffic was light, and they sped through the beautiful Illinois countryside pointing out the red barns and silver silos that had become fixtures in the landscape. Snowy fields stubbled with broken cornstalks stretched for miles. As they neared the city limits, Jennie was astonished at the changes that had occurred in their absence. The latest fast food chains had replaced the feed stores and tractor sales lots. The town's appearance of affluence and abundance replaced the economically-depressed rural life of the 1960's. In the distance they could see tall, white towers and the glittering wires of a new power plant. Turning off the highway, they slowly drove through town past expansive gas stations, rows of brick apartment complexes, glassed-in office buildings and a new subdivision with expensive houses, until they reached the familiar street.

"Oh, this is nice; I like the soft grey-green siding and black shutters," Jennie commented as they pulled into the driveway. Lynn and Roger had told them about the renovation project that included a new entrance and a bay window that changed the front of the house. It all started with the removal of a towering silver maple that had been planted too close to the house, rotting the shingles on that section of the house. Instead of merely replacing the shingles, they added a dormer that altered the elevation and led to one thing and then another. The finishing touch was a new paint job.

Lynn was still the pretty blonde of their college days, and Roger was as tall and straight as ever. After they warmly greeted each other, Tom commented on the changes they had observed as they approached the town. Roger indicated that Quincy had doubled its population in the past ten years, and it had become a booming metropolis. "Of course, the cost of living, taxes, etc. have doubled also. The farmland west of town has been transformed into a gated golf course community. You wouldn't recognize the area! Quincy is not just another small town in Illinois!"

Jennie asked about her family home, and Lynn replied, "Our old neighborhood of 1920's style homes with white picket fences have been torn down and replaced by large mansions. We are amazed that so many people can afford those stately homes."

"Yes, I know," Jennie said, "It's happening all over the Chicago area too. Hinsdale is now known as the 'teardown capital of the US'."

Roger quickly pointed out, "We aren't complaining -- my business has increased twofold. It's just a different way of life."

Their conversations continued throughout dinner, and after they had enjoyed a perfectly roasted turkey and ate all the gourmet sweet potatoes, Jennie and Tom had to bid their hosts good bye. Lynn and

Roger promised they would not become strangers and would visit them soon. They stopped for gas under the bright shelter of a Shell station outside Quincy, ready to join the constant night traffic on I-55 back to Chicago.

Chapter Nine

Christmas baking, Christmas decorations and shopping kept Jennie occupied and away from her desk. "The book can wait," she said, "I have to get everything ready for Charlie and Peggy." Having them come home with their friends was all that she wanted this Christmas. They knew Charlie's girlfriend was Lisa Flanagan, and she was from California, but that's all they knew. Tom said, "I'm glad she's Irish, at least her name would imply." Jennie freshened the guest room with scented soaps and creamy moisture lotions, all the feminine flourishes girls love.

Is Lisa the one we will have to share with Charlie? Is he bringing her home for our blessing? Those thoughts went through Jennie's mind as she anxiously prepared for this special Christmas.

They decided to go "all out" on decorations. Professional decorators showed up with ladders, and greenery and ribbons and transformed the entire house. There were evergreen swags with big red velvet ribbons hanging throughout the large house. There were two large trees that reached to the ceiling – one in the great room and the other in the foyer, and the fireplace mantels were heaped with pine boughs and garland. The tree in the great room was laden with Christopher Radko ornaments, and the tree in the foyer glistened and sparkled with gold and silver ornaments.

Hugs and cheery calls of Merry Christmas filled the foyer as Charlie and Lisa rushed to greet Jennie. Tom had picked them up at the airport. "Mom, this is Lisa Flanagan", and a self-confident, pretty girl thrust her hand forward. Jennie was taken aback by the cheerful, little pixie in tight red crushed-velvet pants whose amber eyes were outlined with black kohl and her high cheekbones set off with blush. She didn't need those enhancements, but it was the style. Her dreadlocks and the tattoo on her left arm set her apart from the rest of the family, but they ignored them, and soon they were all talking at once as if they had been together for years. Then they knew why Charlie liked this beautiful, smart girl.

Peggy was next to arrive, and her comment was, "Home never felt better."

They piled in the Volvo and attended church services. Fine snow had begun to fall, and they parked the van and walked toward the sound of Christmas carols coming from the church. Then they returned home and made a fire in the fireplace and turned on the Christmas tree lights. After a midnight supper, they settled in to the serious business of opening gifts, exclaiming over each one.

At dinner the next day, Lisa was dressed in a rich, red velvet long-sleeved top over white jeans though it was December, and Charlie was wearing a soft red pullover sweater over a white Oxford button-down shirt.

Peggy said, "I like your sweater – is it new?"

"Yes, it was a gift from Lisa."

She thought, *They must be serious. I wouldn't give a guy an expensive cashmere sweater unless he had made a commitment. It has to be a Ralph Lauren or a Michael Kors!*

Lisa's long earrings in the shape of leaves dangled from her pierced ears and flew from side to side as she became animated when discussing the student protests at Berkeley that seemed was more important than her studies at the time. Charlie quietly sat back in admiration as the conversation revolved around her.

Peggy watched in awe of this slightly older, openly-expressive young woman as she described her years at Berkeley where she spent hours making protest posters, circulating petitions, going to rallies and enduring tear gas during the protests for women's rights. She was thoroughly consumed with the issues of the times. After graduation from the University of California she went to the Silicon Valley where she worked with a high tech corporation that developed software. They discussed her job as manager of a software development team. It became evident that she made as much or more money than Charlie, but Jennie and Tom knew they could handle that.

Peggy wanted to know how her brother and this obviously-different girl got to know each other, so she asked Charlie, "How did you and Lisa meet?"

"We met at a campus concert. She wasn't with a date and neither was I. We were both standing alone as if we were lost strangers. At once, we felt that we had to reach out to each other. I smiled at her, and we began conversing as if we had been together for years." Charlie put his arm on the back of her chair. "I discovered she was interesting and she was smart. Right away we trusted each other and we began dating. Soon we were inseparable."

Lisa nodded and added, "He looked like a lonely boy with sad eyes, and I was immediately drawn to him. I was quickly taken in by his charm, his intelligence, and his humor."

Charlie put his arm around her and lightly kissed her cheek.

Jennie wanted to look over at Tom to see his reaction, but it would have been evident, so she kept her thoughts to herself.

At times, Steve also seemed in awe of this outspoken young woman and everyone let her do the talking. Then the subject turned to football, and Steve became the center of attention. Tom and Jennie promised to attend the games on parent's day and homecoming next year. They talked about his studies and his architecture major.

Charlie asked, "Why architecture?"

"I've been drawing buildings since I was two years old. Seriously, I like figuring out how to use space, how can you use it better, are you going to live in it, work in it or play in it, and what are the best and most practical materials. I want to work with Dad in the family construction business, and then we'll be able to offer a complete design-build package. It's called D & B, sort of a one-stop shopping concept. I'll do the design, and he'll handle the building and construction, all under one roof."

Peggy chimed in, "And I'll do the decorating."

Steve looked surprised and smiled approvingly.

Peggy blushed at the implication of her remark and then told everyone about her interior design studies.

When everyone had their fill of the delicious turkey dinner, Lisa followed Jennie into the kitchen where she took over loading the dishwasher and cleaning the counters. Peggy followed unable to take her eyes off Lisa as she took over the kitchen duties with complete ease. Peggy served the coffee, Jennie served pumpkin pie with whipped cream, and the conversations resumed.

The entire weekend was an entertaining sequence of events. The day after Christmas the kids left to spend time with their friends, and Jennie and Tom returned to their routine, and, of course, they had the opportunity to size up Lisa and Charlie's relationship.

Jennie said, "I just can't imagine Charlie and Lisa in a long term relationship like marriage which is supposed to be forever."

"They are two different personalities, but they seem to get along well," Tom replied.

"I hope Charlie doesn't fall madly in love and then be tossed aside like an old shoe."

"If dissension does arise, I think they will become aware of their differences long before anyone gets hurt. Let's not concoct a scenario that doesn't exist. Why don't we go out to eat tonight?"

"Yes, let's, I'll call Suz, maybe they could meet us at Tony's."

*****

Charlie and Lisa flew back to New York after Christmas as Lisa had to be back at work. Peggy was riding with Steve, and they had a few extra days before classes resumed. Peggy looked forward to spending time alone with her parents. At her first opportunity, she asked, "So what did you think of Lisa?"

Jennie said, "I thought she was attractive, smart and fun to be with."

"Yes, but I wish she'd do something with her hair. Nobody does dreadlocks anymore. She looked like she never left Berkeley."

"Well, computers and software were developed by some brilliant geeks who started that look, so she fits in with her business," Tom commented.

"Did you notice that poor Charlie didn't have a chance to say a word – he'll probably turn into a wimp."

"Peggy, I think you're being a little hard on Lisa. Charlie didn't take over the conversation because he wanted Lisa to get to know us, and when you're a teacher and you hear yourself talking all day, there are times when you want to let someone else do the talking. That's why your mother does all the talking around here."

Jennie abruptly turned to look at him and comment and then saw him wink. "You're trouble!" she said.

"It's good to see women excel in business, and Lisa does have a very good job. When I was growing up, women stayed home watching the house and the kids; and they were bored and lonely. That's how it was in those days, before women spoke out, before the changes. I think we should be glad she took part in those protests," Jennie said."Both of you are right. I do like her, and I'm a little jealous of her.

Chapter Ten

Another time when Charlie came home, Jennie was in her office totally engrossed in what she was doing and didn't hear him enter. He asked her what held her interest so intently. She told him she was working on her seventh book.

"Mom, I admire the way you have stuck to writing. Most people lose interest in projects and end up saying they wished they would have done this or wished they would have done that."

"Well, Charlie, I sincerely wanted to be a successful writer, and one has to 'stick with it' if they want to succeed."

Then she looked over at the bookcase and pointed to six books side-by-side on a shelf and said, "On this shelf are nine inches of my life's work, but I'm reaching the stage in my life when I want to slow down. It's time-consuming and tiring. Writing is a solitary occupation, and at times a lonely existence."

"I'm impressed with your success, Mom, but I think you are wise; you and Dad should be enjoying life more instead of working so hard."

"I'm all for that, but your father wants another career. He retired from Kellogg at the age of 60 after teaching for 35 years, earning him the title of Professor Emeritus, but his educator's pension doesn't always reach far enough. He plans to continue writing, and he has joined The Speaker's Platform. As a result, he will be required to travel extensively for speaking engagements. Some engagements will take him abroad A perk for me is that I will be able to accompany him on his travels. When he started talking about retirement, I was petrified that I would have to follow him to an over fifty-five community in Florida or Arizona."

Charlie smiled and said, "I can't see either of you in Florida or Arizona. I'm not surprised that he would join Speaker's Platform; I know how much he likes his soapbox. When he gets started on something, it's like he never wants to quit. I hope I can be as devoted as he is."

"Charlie, you are just like your father. I'm happy that Peggy finally knows what she wants to do. She's artistic, and she wants to be an Interior Designer. She plans to work for a design firm for a year before taking her licensing exam. She also wants to get her bachelor of architectural degree. Then she'll want to re-do the whole house – by that time it will probably need it."

"Our lives won't be as busy as it sounds. We will still walk the beach and then rest and reflect to refuel. We both get energized from the endless expanse of Lake Michigan. Water invigorates our senses and allows our minds to wander."

"But what about you and Lisa? Are you planning to marry soon?"

"Yes, that's what I wanted to talk to you about. Of course, the wedding will be in Santa Barbara where her parents, Silva and Richard, are living. They have separated, but they both still live there. The date is July 21st, and it will take place at 4 o'clock in the chapel at the First Congregational Church. The reception will be at Montecito Country Club. Lisa and her mother have been making all the plans by phone. It's going to be very small – Lisa's sister, Linda, and her husband, Jack Seagrave, will be our attendants. Then we'll leave immediately for Cape Cod. That will be our honeymoon."

"We're looking at a house on the Cape to have as a weekend getaway and a vacation home. We put a bid on it as did three others so cross your fingers that we'll get it. We both love the Cape and want to spend as much time there as possible. The house is in Barnstable on Millway Beach. It's an old year-around home, but it's in good condition. Of course, we'll probably make some changes. We preferred to buy in the upscale community of Oyster Point, but when this home came on the market, we fell in love with it, and since it was move-in ready, we quickly dismissed all thoughts of Oyster Point. We wanted to get married there, but Lisa's parents want her to come home to California to be married."

"Charlie, that sounds wonderful, I've always loved Cape Cod, and I'm happy to hear you'll be marrying soon. The wedding in Santa Barbara sounds lovely. Your father will be pleased, too."

"Lisa already has plans for Christmas next year. Her parents divorced when she was seventeen and then went their separate ways. There were never any Christmases or family get-togethers, so our Christmas was the best one she's had in years. She wants us to start a Christmas tradition after we are married, so be prepared to come East for the holiday. It'll be a trade-off; we'll come here for Thanksgiving and you'll have Christmas with us."

"That will be fine, Charlie. Your father and I are well aware of the concessions that must be made when their children leave home and marry. Besides, I've always been partial to Thanksgiving with everyone sitting around a table groaning with food."

"Lisa decided that we should combine our belongings and live in my redbrick row house near the Columbia campus. Lisa's corporate headquarters are in Manhattan, and she had an apartment on the Upper East Side. She loved the glitz and glamour of the area, but, of course, it's expensive. When we talked about buying property on the Cape, she decided we should live together to save money. You're in for a surprise when you see my house now."

Jennie was surprised at Charlie's admission that they were living together and especially that it was Lisa's idea. *Oh well, they are adults, and they do plan to marry. I wonder what Tom will say… There's nothing we can do about it...*

Lisa's colorful, contemporary art brightened the bare walls, and her collection of blue-and-white Chinese export ware blended well with Charlie's leather couch, faded Tunisian rugs and built-in bookcases that were crammed with books that overflowed to stacks on the floor. It was evident that his favorite haunt was the Barnes & Noble store a few blocks away. Her round dining room table with antique chairs replaced Charlie's folding card table in the dining area. Everything was artfully arranged now. Anything that wouldn't fit in Charlie's row house would be taken to the house on the Cape.

Charlie and Lisa's bid was the winner, and after they closed on the house, they eagerly turned the key in the weathered oak door and a rush of warm, stale air hit their faces. The house and front porch had received a fresh coat of white paint, and the front lawn that consisted of sparse salt grass sloped downward to the beach and ocean.. Even though the house had been empty for months, it was surprisingly clean. It only needed love and attention. The old-money family that had owned it for forty years had passed on, and either the newer generation had not wanted it, or they were not able to afford it.

The great room ran the length of the front of the house with a row of windows extending from one side to the other. They walked toward the windows and were entranced by the gently churning gray-green water that would be their everyday view. A bedroom, kitchen, and powder room were in the rear of the great room, and the second story consisted of four bedrooms and full bath. It was more space than Charlie and Lisa needed now, but soon it would be overflowing as friends and family joined them for fun in the sun on weekends.

With the castoff furniture and dishes from their homes in the city, their summer home on the Cape began to take shape. The wooden floors were old and scarred from years of use, but they were waxed and polished. Several faded throw rugs were scattered about. The stone fireplace gave off a musky smell. The kitchen with red-striped wallpaper was bare except for a 1940's red Formica dinette set with four chairs. The house belonged to another time, but they loved it. With a fire burning in the fireplace, it would be warm and cozy.

Lisa indicated that she would not change the kitchen, and it may become her favorite room in the house. The white cabinets blended well with the red-striped wallpaper and the retro red Formica table and chairs. We quickly sensed her penchant for red and white and red in particular. It appeared to be her favorite color, and there were touches of red throughout the house.

There wasn't anything they didn't like about the house, even the sloping floors in the bedrooms, the shallow closets, the windows with old-fashioned storms that had to be painstakingly put up each fall and taken off each spring, but when cleaned were as beautiful as the view outside. Sometimes it was an effort to pull away from the view when there were chores at hand.

The first items they purchased were a grill, lounge chairs with red pillows, and little wicker tables for the patio so they could sit and watch the white waves gently moving over the sand. From the patio, they could run to the sandy beach and brave the white curdled waves of the sea. In the morning they would awaken to the sound of the pounding surf and the shrill cry of sea gulls. On Friday after work they'd rush home and take off for the Cape. To not lose precious time they packed their bags the night before.

*****

The glare of the sun that reflected from the passing cars blinded her momentarily. The phone rang, and she moved away from the window to take the call.

"Good morning, Matt. I'm glad you called. I've been working on 'The Sequel,' and I was wondering if you would go over my draft of the first few chapters. Bear in mind it's my memoir, not fiction. I'm having trouble with the viewpoint, I keep going from first to third person, and I'd like your input before proceeding. If you're too busy, just say so."

"No, I'm not too busy, Jen, I'd love to read it. A lot has been happening in your life so I'm sure it's interesting. I'll stop over tonight and pick up your manuscript, or on second thought, are you and Tom free for dinner at Tony's?"

"Yes, that would be fun. Suz and I haven't seen each other for at least a week. Can we meet at 6?"

"That will be perfect. See you at 6."

"So what do you hear from Lauren?" Jennie asked after they had been seated.

"Oh, not good," Suzanne replied, and Jennie and Tom abruptly looked up from their menus expecting to hear that something dreadful happened to her in Africa where she is serving with the Peace Corps.

"She was scheduled to come home this month but instead she re-upped or signed on for another five years. She says the people need her. It didn't matter that I told her I needed her, too."

"Suz, I know you desperately miss her, but you must realize that Lauren is a compassionate person who truly wants to help those poor people. She is a true humanitarian."

"Yes, I know, and I don't know where she gets it from, but five more years is a long time. We won't have seen her for ten years. Will we even know her, what will she look like? At times I can't bear to think about it," her voice breaking. "And, we worry about her. When you have to live in a house surrounded by a high wall and barbed wire, it's difficult to not worry. The Peace Corp volunteers are all young American kids filled with energy and sacrifice. They don't worry about themselves; their only concern is the people they are there to help."

"You, too, were a liberal idealist when you were young, remember?" Jennie commented.

"Yes, I know, but its different being over there."

Matt put his arm around her, and his eyes began to glass over. He needed to be consoled, too.

"Don't they usually get some time off between assignments, a furlough so to speak?" Tom asked.

"Yes, she will be coming home for a week, but it's the long haul that we don't like. Five more years is a long time, but we have to accept our daughter's decision – it's her life, and she's doing what she wants to do. She's an adult, and we have to get used to her leading her own life."

"I used to worry about Peggy, but now that she's grown and knows what she wants to do, I don't worry so much." Wishing she could take back that rather banal remark, Jennie made the suggestion that they order two different pizzas and split them.

"That's a good idea," Matt said. "Everyone for a Bud Light?"

Chapter Eleven

Tom accepted a speaking engagement that took him to the U.S. Chamber of Commerce headquarters in Washington, D.C. He had been invited to speak at a Small Business Seminar, and his topic was "Our Place in the World Economy."

Jennie stood on the podium in her new navy suit and Prada pumps looking out at the sea of attendees as Tom was being introduced to the press. He stood at a lectern beside the American flag, and she was close to being overcome from the pride she felt for him. After he acknowledged the applause, she moved back and took her seat as Tom addressed the crowd. "Ladies and Gentlemen, I don't need to tell any of you of the vital importance…"

Her mind wandered back to the evening they met at Tony's in Lincoln Park. Tony's was the hangout for the up and coming young professionals in the area, and she and Suzanne were frequent customers. They were both single then, and Jennie had just returned from spending the weekend in Quincy. Suzanne had called and told her she wanted to introduce her to a wonderful man. It was love at first sight, and their love for each other has endured for twenty-five years. Two children later, they are still actively pursuing new interests.

Now the applause from the audience rose, and the cameramen jostled for their close-ups. He leaned closer to the microphone to thank the crowd, and it was the end of another speaking engagement. She loved traveling with Tom and being a part of his new business venture.

Since it was November, and they hadn't seen Charlie and Lisa's summer home on the Cape, they thought it would be fun to fly to Boston and rent a car and drive to Barnstable. Then it occurred to them they could celebrate Thanksgiving at the Cape. Peggy and Steve, if he was able to join them, would fly to Boston and drive with Jennie and Tom to the Cape. They would shop for groceries, and Jennie and Tom would prepare their turkey dinner there. They would all enjoy a Thanksgiving feast while looking out at the pounding surf and watching squawking sea gulls dive into the water for their own feast.

They drove to Ralph's Market that at one time had been a glorified convenience store with creaking wooden floors and a single cash register, but it now rivaled the Whole Foods where she shopped at home. Tom grabbed a shopping cart and they proceeded up and down aisles filling it with a frozen turkey big enough to feed a village, two kinds of potatoes, frozen corn and fresh broccoli, and eggs and bread for breakfast. Peggy went to find the cranberries and some Stilton and Brie cheese and crackers for snacking. Steve's contribution to the cart was bagels, spinach dip, and carrots and celery. Tom said he needed enough celery and onion for the dressing and some brown sugar to glaze the sweet potatoes, and he made a second trip to the dairy section for butter, milk and juice. Before leaving, he steered the cart to the wine department for both red and white wine as Peggy said she gets headaches from red wine.

After unloading the brimming cart, they wended their way through town, past mostly capes and colonials that gave Millway Beach what charm it had. Most were summer homes for people from the city. In the distance, scrub pine dotted the dunes, along side coastal salt ponds and marshes. They made a right turn and the neighborhood began to thin out and patches of salt marsh separated one house from another. They were on the ocean frontage road, and they continued to skirt the beach until they came to a white Cape Cod with black shutters and a mailbox with the name "Doyle" neatly printed on it. The home stood on a hill, giving it a magnificent view of the endless expanse of ocean.

Tom turned up the heat, and they staked out their bedrooms upstairs. The beds had been made and enormous white towels were hanging in the bathroom in anticipation of their visit. Jennie unpacked the food and put it away while Tom put the frozen turkey in water in the sink to begin the thawing process. Then they put on their coats and went for a walk to explore the beach.

Later in the evening as they were engrossed in a game of Scrabble, headlights flashed light through the front windows and car doors slammed. Charlie and Lisa burst into the room with hugs for all. They had left work early and then left immediately for the Cape.

On Thanksgiving morning Peggy studied the table she had just set with six place settings of blue and white dishes and blue glasses. She was pleased that the glasses sparkled from the sunshine streaking through the front windows. She knew the effect wouldn't last, so she lingered to admire her creation.

A fire was crackling in the fireplace in the great room and smells of turkey and dressing wafted from the kitchen. Tom and Jennie had gotten up early to put the turkey in the oven, and now Peggy and Lisa set up a side table containing the cheeses and vegetables and dip along with glasses for wine, beer or Coke.

Steve and Charlie, both dressed in khaki pants and sweaters, were checking the TV guide for the lineup of football games to watch. They each had their favorite teams so the games could last well into the evening. They had brought in an ample supply of fireplace wood to chase away the evening chill.

Lisa and Peggy vowed that they would need to take a long walk to walk off some calories. They had become close friends and could easily have been taken for sisters. Lisa had long ago abandoned her dreadlocks and had let her silky brown hair grow to its shoulder length identical to Peggy's hair style. Lisa said she was letting her hair grow for her wedding.

After an hour of snacking, Tom carved the turkey, first separating the drumsticks from the thighs and then slicing the white meat on the breasts.

He said a short prayer; "Lord, we give you thanks that we're all healthy and together. Please bless this meal and all of us."

"Save me a drumstick," Steve called out as the platter of turkey was being passed around.

After seconds and groans of over-indulgence, Jennie suggested they walk the beach and have coffee and dessert while watching football. Everyone approved, and they hastily cleared the table before heading out the door.

Instead of watching football, the girls gathered around the dining room table with their coffee. Jennie asked Lisa what she could do to help with their wedding plans, and Lisa told her they needed a guest list for the invitations that were being printed.

"I'll start working on that this weekend. Tom and I will want to invite Matt and Suzanne; Lauren is in Africa with the Peace Corps so that leaves her out, but Linda and Roger Smith in Quincy may be able to attend. They've known Charlie since he was born. Tom will want to invite a fellow professor and his wife, and I'll probably think of a few others. Peggy, do you want to invite Steve? If the wedding was being held in Chicago, it would be easier to add to the list, but as it is, our list will be small."

"I understand. Because of the distance to Santa Barbara, we are planning a small wedding. Mom has been great, she is taking over completely. All Charlie and I will have to do is show up. I'm going to shop for my dress after the holidays."

They sat around the fire until the last log fell down in a shower of embers and ash. It had been a wonderful Thanksgiving with her family in a cozy house by the ocean, and now she knew why Charlie and Lisa so desperately wanted this home on the Cape. Jennie had no doubts about their future together, and she envisioned coming here on vacations and holding a grandchild's hand while walking the beach, stopping now and then to pick up shells and sea glass.

They all returned to New York for Christmas in Charlie and Lisa's redbrick row house in Morningside Heights. It was a festive Christmas amid the city lights and traffic noises. Lisa's parents flew in from California. They dressed and dined out, completely different from the casual Thanksgiving celebration at the Cape, but Lisa told of her future plans for a huge Christmas tree filling a window in the great room, shining as a welcoming beacon to all who came to celebrate Christmas at the Cape.

*****

Chapter Twelve

Jennie and Tom's New Year started off with a speaking engagement in mid-January at Case Western Reserve University in Cleveland, Ohio. They decided to drive since the roads were clear and they had plenty of time. They skipped breakfast and got an early start. Weak sunshine was starting to filter through the clouds in the early morning hours. Traffic on I-90 was light and they made good time. Signs advertising the Sunshine Café at the next exit reminded them that they hadn't eaten breakfast so they pulled off the Interstate at a small town near the Ohio border. It was a typical small town diner, and the parked semi's with their diesel engines idling in the parking lot suggested it was a truck stop.

When they entered, Jennie thought it was a place right out of a southern novel, as she mentally made a note of the trucker's loud conversations competing with Neil Diamond singing Sweet Caroline, sunshine streaming through limp curtains that half covered the large expanse of windows, bright lime green paint that she imagined seeing on the close-out table at the local hardware store covered the walls, the stools at the counter covered in bright red leather, black and white floor tiles faded and worn thin from heavy boots and stiletto heels, and the wonderful aroma of warm bread and hamburgers sizzling on the grill. The lone waitress quickly moved from table to booth balancing a heavy tray of food, then paused to stop and take another order.

The manager, with a small black mustache, wore a polyester short-sleeved shirt and a clip-on tie. He grabbed a couple of menus from the counter and rushed to them. "Good morning," he said as he showed them to the only available booth. They leafed through the laminated menus with color photos of eggs sunny side up, blueberry waffles, crisp green salads, and apple pie ala mode too delicious to resist.

Jennie said, "This looks like a Perkins menu."

"It does; I thought it looked familiar. I know what I want," and he set the menu aside without looking at it.

Jennie continued to study the menu remarking that "everything looked so good."

"I'll wager that most women order from the pictures instead of reading the menu."

"Yes, I guess we respond more to our visual senses than men, and we like to try different things."

"I'll admit I'm not very adventuresome when it comes to breakfast."

The manager returned with glasses of water and asked, "Ready to order?"

"Everything looks so good. I'll have the blueberry waffles," Jennie replied.

He turned to Tom, and Tom said, "Make it two eggs up and whole wheat toast. We'll both have black coffee."

A young trucker with long sideburns got up from his booth to feed the jukebox, and Elvis was crooning "Are You Lonesome Tonight" as the manager set a pot of coffee and heavy plates of steaming food before them.

A half hour later they were back on the road, and the weather was good until they neared Toledo. A cold wind was blowing off Lake Erie and weather reports on the radio were warning travelers of an ice storm coming off the lake. They continued on and kept the radio tuned to the news and weather station. As they neared Cleveland, the forecaster indicated that a blizzard and major freeze was bearing down on the Cleveland area, and he further stated, "Heavy snow will be accompanied by high winds making for life-threatening conditions if not properly prepared. Travel will become impossible at times on local roadways and the Interstate. Snow drifts will range between 4 and 8 feet in some locations. Visibility will be reduced considerably during the height of the snow and wind." They advised parents to stay tuned for school closings. It started to rain a freezing rain, and Tom had the wipers on top speed but they weren't taking the ice from the windshield. "Damn," he said, "These wipers are shot. I should have replaced them a month ago when they weren't working properly. We are in for some real difficult driving conditions." The Interstate had become a treacherous ribbon of black ice.

They drove cautiously and soon they were within the city limits searching for their motel. They tried to read the street signs through the icy build-up on the windshield, but they were forced to pull over to check their map and put the defrosters on full blast. The freezing rain had turned to snow, and it was snowing heavily. They drove slowly as traffic got heavier, and at each stoplight the car skidded to a shaky stop. The streets were a sheet of ice, and the snow wasn't just getting thicker, it was sticking, wet and heavy. The wipers were barely working.

The wind grew stronger, 55 miles per hour with 60 mile per hour gusts, and the snow which was now becoming more granular, was blowing horizontally making visibility extremely difficult. Tom had to rely on the taillights of vehicles ahead to guide the way. The wipers were on high, and the defroster was going full blast in an effort to keep the windshield clear. Jennie tried to read the street signs, but the signs had been zapped with snow and it had stuck to them. The swirling snowfall was so thick the buildings on either side of the street looked like gray hulks huddled together for protection against the storm. They crept along in silence as if conversation would impair their vision.

Suddenly, Jennie spotted the familiar green and gold sign shining like a beacon in the blurry landscape, and she cried out, "There it is, the Holiday Inn, it's up in the next block." "Thank, God," Tom said, "I don't think I could take much more of this." They cautiously made their way toward the sign and inched along hoping they were turning into the parking lot entrance as it was difficult to see where it was. Several cars behind followed them into the parking lot seeking refuge from the storm. The Holiday Inn would become a safe haven from the raging storm.

When Tom brought the car to a stop, he rested his head on the steering wheel, and breathed a sigh of relief. They walked on wobbly legs until the tension eased and they were able to relax. As they were checking in, the man at the desk said, "We are in a weather front straight from the Arctic. The Mayor has closed down everything but essential services. It's going to be way below zero for three days at least. Guess you folks will be staying with us for awhile. Make yourself at home in the bar and restaurant."

"Great!" Tom muttered. When they were in their room, he tried calling his contact at Case Western, and was told that everyone had left because of the storm. The man who answered the phone checked the seminar schedule and told Tom it read, "Seminar canceled (to be rescheduled in May)."

Tom was both relieved and disappointed, and Jennie tried to console him. Then they started laughing at the situation: Snowbound at the Holiday Inn in Cleveland, Ohio. "We might as well make the best of it. I could use a drink, let's go see if the cook is here," Tom said.

After dinner, Jennie and Tom returned to their room to watch television and relax. The television newscasters stated that Cleveland was paralyzed by a storm. All businesses closed, flights were cancelled, schools closed, and people were advised to stay home until the emergency was over. Jennie called Charlie and Peggy to let them know they were safe and well. Next, she called Suzanne, and they laughed and joked about the fun they were having in Cleveland, Ohio.

The storm finally abated and after spending two days at the motel playing cards and visiting with the other guests, they set out for Chicago and home. The major highways had been cleared, and although it was bitter cold, the sun was shining brightly. Driving down the streets was like driving through a tunnel with the high banks of snow on either side. The snow crunched under their wheels until they reached the interstate where the road was clear.

When they arrived at home, Tom checked in at Case Western, and his seminar was rescheduled to May 22nd. Apologies were profuse due to the suddenness of the storm and their inability to reach him.

Chapter Thirteen

Spring came, and sadness entered Jennie's life. Her dear friend, Lynn Smith, became ill from the flu, and pneumonia set in. Her untimely death at an early age was devastating. Jennie asked why Lynn became infected and why the antibiotics had no affect on the bacterial infection, but her questions went unanswered. The doctors didn't know why one individual can be overwhelmed by the bacteria while another infected by the same microbe recovers rather quickly.

While being hospitalized, Roger was the only person allowed to visit her, and she died before Jennie could see her. She wasn't able to say good-bye or tell her once again that she loved her. Hers was another unsaid farewell. First, there was Steve, then her mother, and now Lynn, three people she treasured dearly. Roger was overcome with grief. They felt so sorry for him – he looked gaunt and grey as he went through the rituals of the funeral. The Presbyterian Church overflowed with mourners, and the Ladies Aid served lunch after the eleven o'clock service.

They went with Roger to the cemetery where Lynn was laid to rest, and they stood at her grave for a long time, thinking of her and the pleasure she brought to their lives. They found a sense of closure in being there. As they left, the sun came out and big puffy clouds were slowly moving about. They imagined it was a farewell gesture.

Afterward they went home with Roger so he wouldn't be alone. Roger and Lynn Smith were well known in Quincy since they owned the State Farm Insurance Agency, and Jennie thought other people would have the same thought. She went to the kitchen and stared at the long, granite counter which was covered with dishes of food – casseroles, salads, pies, entire dinners in separately marked plastic containers, brownies, cakes, cookies, and two bright pink Dunkin' Donuts boxes and a package of Styrofoam coffee cups. It would take a large family days to eat all of that!

"It's what people do," Roger said. "They don't know what else to do, so they bring food."

The doorbell rang, and the words, "how deeply sorry" drifted to the kitchen. Jennie and Tom began making coffee and preparing the food for a buffet. They took plates from the cabinets, directed the guests who were coming one after another to be with Roger, to take a plate, help themselves, and go to the dining room. In no time the table that sat twelve was crowded to capacity. The conversation that began in short, hushed tones, gradually rose in volume, and then there was laughter. Jennie saw Roger's face light up, and his downcast eyes began to twinkle with laughter.

Everyone noticed Roger's transformation, and they continued to eat and converse because they wanted to linger and stay close to him. They ate as if it was a chore that had to be accomplished, and in no time the counter was spread with empty dishes. In early evening when the last ray of sunshine disappeared in the horizon, they began to trickle out the door. They hugged and kissed Roger, promising they would get together again soon. No one said the word "good-bye" realizing that it could trigger a quick jolt of sadness.

Roger insisted that Jennie and Tom stay overnight, and they gratefully accepted his offer. The four-hour drive back to Chicago could wait until tomorrow

*****

Since finishing school and getting her degree, Peggy looked at everything with a critical eye. She had taken a job with an interior decorating firm in Chicago, and she was anxious to put her name on something, so Jennie and Tom gave her full rein with the family home.

"Mother, the carpeting has to go, wall-to-wall carpeting is out of style and it has a traffic pattern. You need to update this room. There is probably hardwood flooring underneath so you won't have that expense, but they will need to be sanded and polished. We'll go to the Merchandise Mart and look for a large area rug."

Jennie knew it would be futile to rebel. Peggy had just become the family decorator, and she knew this wouldn't be the first change. But she did agree that the worn carpeting in the living room was out of date, and since Peggy said "we'll" go to the Merchandise Mart, she would consent to a new area rug. She even thought it would be an exciting venture and looked forward to the transformation.

"The rest of the rooms will only need editing; repainting, reupholstering, and new drapes or blinds, etc."

"Those are things you can redo if needed, however, the mural in the dining room is off limits, I do not want that altered in any way."

"I agree, Mom, the mural has to remain as is."

"But everything will have to wait until after the wedding. Will you help me shop for my dress. Maybe I should find out what Silva will be wearing so the mother of the bride and the mother of the groom will not look like twins."

"I'd love to shop with you. Steve is going on an architectural tour to Galena with his friend, Ben Jordan, and they'll be gone all weekend."

*****

Steve and Ben left Chicago on I-90 to Rockford, then took Hwy 20 past Freeport and the Chestnut Mountain Ski Resort which was in a heavily wooded area near Galena. Their destination was Galena, an old mining town along the Mississippi River. It was the home of General Ulysses Grant, and it was well known for other distinctive homes of architectural significance. Each spring the Chamber of Commerce hosted a tour of its famous residences, and Steve was anxious to attend the tour.

Around six-thirty in the evening they were driving through the dusky countryside around the ski resort. A red fox was trotting through the woods alongside the road, and they were alerted to the honking of geese enroute to the nearby pond. Suddenly a deer bolted and jumped out of the woods, running and leaping in front of their car. Steve was in the passenger's seat, and with a loud thunk the deer slammed onto the car. Ben hit the brakes, but the huge deer crashed onto the hood and through the front window hitting Steve and knocking him unconscious. Ben fought the wheel as they skidded into the opposite lane. No one heard his scream as the car was spinning and gaining speed with each revolution. Then the car shot backward down a steep, rocky embankment. Within minutes, Steve was gone, his face torn open.

Peggy choked back angry tears as Steve's closed casket was wheeled to the front of the church. The prayers, the hymns, the 23rd Psalm all blurred together; then she was leaving the church. She remembered it all, but she wasn't there. Her mind was back in time. She inhaled deeply as they left the church and stepped out into the crisp fall air. It seemed to clear her head, and she was able to think clearer.

"Mom, I loved him."

"I know you did. I loved him, too. We all loved him," Jennie replied.

"Why did this have to happen?"

"Don't dwell on the why," Jennie said. "There is no why. It doesn't matter, it doesn't help. Putting her arm around her shoulder, she said, "Honey, you're exhausted, let's go home."

"I'm all right, but I need time by myself."

Peggy fingered Steve's class ring that once was a promise for their future. Then with a fury, she hurled the ring against the far wall of her bedroom. The past was a cruel memory, and their future was forfeited by screeching metal and smashing glass. That stupid deer. Why did it have to run out in front of his car? The scene continued to play in her head, and sometimes the deer's wide eyes were staring at her pleading for forgiveness.

Tom went to Peggy's room to be with her. He didn't think it was right that she sealed herself off from everyone. When he talked to her there was silence. Finally Peggy told him she just needed to be by herself. He left and went to Jennie, she needed consoling, too.

"Peggy's fine, she needs to rest for a few days, just watch videos, and eat popcorn. It's like a drug, and she needs it for as long as she feels this way. She needs to heal, Jennie."

"But I'd like to be with her," Jennie protested.

"You've been with her every minute of every day for four days. By your presence, you're tearing each other apart. You can't bear her grief, and she can't bear to think of how much you're hurting. You don't normally spend time with her like that."

"This isn't normally."

"Well, maybe we need to get back to normal as much as possible. Peggy will when she's ready."

Two days later, Peggy stood in front of her mirror and was shocked by her appearance. Her eyes were swollen from crying and her lustrous brown hair had lost its shine and it hung lifeless around her face. She'd had a headache since early morning so she swallowed several Tylenol tablets without counting. She couldn't imagine surviving another day like the ones she had been through. She had cried so much she thought her head would split. She knew she needed more time to heal, but she needed to get away from her room and the TV. She flipped it off and went to the bathroom. She gave both knobs a vicious twist; she wanted the rush of water to pelt her skin, she needed to feel something so she'd know she was alive. She let the warm water beat against her body as she shampooed her hair. She had gone through all kinds of emotions, from anger to exhaustion, and now she was ready to face reality again.

After she dressed in her favorite sweater and jeans, she went to Jennie, and said, "Mom, do you want to shop for your dress today?"

Jennie knew the time had come. "Yes, Hon, I'll change clothes and be with you in a minute.

The following day, Steve's friend, Ben Jordan, who was in Steve's architectural class and the driver of the car, called Peggy to ask how she was doing. He told her that a bunch of Steve's friends and their dates were going to Tony's for pizza, just to hang out and be together, and he wanted Peggy to go with him. He told her it would be good for her to get out and talk with friends and even have a good laugh. He said they all needed to do that. He told her she had met or seen most of them at school do she wouldn't be with strangers.

"I'd like that, Ben," she said.

Chapter Fourteen

They boarded the United plane and made their way to the coach section. Tom gestured to Peggy to take the window seat as she always became restless if she didn't have something to divert her attention. Jennie sat in the middle seat. Tom put their carry-ons in the overhead bin. The door to the cockpit was open, and Jennie could see the crew. The size of the cockpit never failed to startle her. Many of them were smaller than the front seat of automobiles. The captain rose and turned toward the cabin. He was an older man with salt and pepper hair, and he seemed almost too kindly to be in charge. Safer than driving a car, Tom always told her. She immediately relaxed. The plane lumbered to the runway. The pilot revved the engines for take-off and then they were airborne. Her heart stalled and beat wildly in her chest until they were in the air. It's always that way, the fear that the plane won't rise. The flight attendants began their routine, and it would be just another daily flight. She pressed her seat back, and Tom aligned his seat with hers. Peggy was entranced with the disappearing scenery as the plane ascended to its cruising altitude. They were on their way to Santa Barbara for the wedding of Charlie Doyle and Lisa Flanagan.

The wedding took place in the First Congregational Church, which was a simple white clapboard church that could have stood on the main street of any small New England village. It was reminiscent of Barnstable on Cape Cod where Charlie and Lisa were anxious to honeymoon for two weeks. The Carillons played a quiet rendition of "For the Beauty of the Earth" as they climbed the steps past guests waiting in line. The ushers escorted them to the front row where Silva and Richard Flanagan had already been seated.

Lisa's bridal gown was an exquisite ivory satin gown with Chantilly lace bodice, a low-cut v-neckline and long sleeves. She wore a crystal tiara with a short, sheer veil. Her father walked her down the aisle that was lined with white Calla lilies. Her sister, Linda who was her maid of honor, wore a sleeveless, long pink satin dress with fitted bodice and low-cut v-neckline. Jennie was gorgeous in a rose colored dress with spaghetti straps, and Lisa's mother wore a similar dress in light green. The ceremony was short and beautiful. Photos were taken afterward.

After the wedding everyone headed to the Monceito Country Club. Jennie, Tom, and Peggy shared a ride with Suzanne and Matt. Cocktails were served on the outdoor terrace set with white tables and chairs, and warm yellow lights were hidden in the trees that surrounded the terrace. Waiters carried trays of hors d'oeuvres and champagne above their shoulders, and a pianist played show tunes.

Lisa's eyes were bright and her smile full of love. She had changed into a chic long black dress, and she wore no jewelry. Any jewelry would have been a distraction. Charlie beamed with pride, and he kept repeating the words "my wife" as in "my wife and I were talking" or "my wife thinks that." He'd mouth those words and smile as if he was savoring the most succulent wine.

Dinner was simple; poached salmon with new potatoes, asparagus spears, an endive and spinach salad, fresh fruit, and croissants, served with a delicious Chardonnay. The four-tiered wedding cake took center stage, beautifully adorned with pink ribbons and fresh flowers, filled with chocolate mousse and covered with butter cream icing. The sweets table also included mocha tortes, assorted mousses, and after-dinner cordials.

The customary toasts were given. Kevin entertained the guests with tales of Charlie's first car, how they washed it every other day, then in a moment that was to be a thrill, he crashed into a tree and totaled it; his dog, Sam; and their hours playing basketball. Lisa's father spoke tenderly of his precocious daughter; then led her to the dance floor where Charlie symbolically cut in, and they danced the first dance cheek to cheek. The partying and dancing continued until midnight, and then the couple said goodbye to their parents and headed for their honeymoon retreat on Cape Cod.

After the wedding, Jennie, Tom and Peggy continued on to Seattle where Tom had a speaking engagement at a Rotary Club convention. He spoke on corporate volunteerism after a delicious dinner at the Space Needle restaurant. The view of city lights at night was a breath-taking galaxy of lights.

Jennie planned to attend the book signing of Joyce Carol Oates' latest book, "We Were the Mulvaneys." Oates had become her favorite author, and she was anxious to meet her and tell her how much she enjoyed her work. Joyce Carol Oates was a brilliant writer, and Jennie was in awe of her success.

When they entered the bookstore, Oates was reading in her deep, warm, singsong voice with a hint of a foreign accent. Swedish, Jennie thought. She looked like a waif standing there so pale, with a voice like a small stringed instrument. She spoke about her deep feeling for her characters and how she spent hours inventing suitable names for them. She spoke about the importance of a character's name and how it affected their role in the story. After the reading, people crowded around, money in hand to purchase a book. As she signed the books, her large, owl-like glasses slipped down on her nose, and she jabbed at them with a slender finger as she asked each person for a name and thanked them for coming. Jennie hung back until the crowd thinned and then introduced herself to Oates. Joyce told Jennie how much she enjoyed her writing, and said that after she had read "A Brief Wondrous Life," she wanted to read everything that Jennie had written. This pleased Jennie to the extent that she felt their meeting almost overshadowed the wedding. Jennie said she learned how different a "public figure" can be from the people we read about in the papers.

*****

The scorching August sun drove everyone to the beach and their vacation homes at the northern lakes, and Tom and Jennie joined them. It had been several years since they had gone to Gull Lake in northern Minnesota. Tom was eager to get out on the lake and fish so once again they drove north for a week of fishing. This vacation was different; it would be just the two of them. She would write while Tom fished like it was before they were married. They took long walks and at sundown cooked the fresh fish and ate outside beneath the pines with the night sounds of crickets and loons communicating with one another.

They reminisced as they sat outside in the refreshing night air enjoying their favorite wine. They thought back to the day when Dr. Kantor surprised them with the news that she was pregnant, and how much joy Peggy had brought to their lives. Now they couldn't imagine their lives without her. Jennie couldn't bear to discard the stick self-portraits in triangle dresses with funny little club feet pointing in the same direction that Peggy drew almost daily saying, "Mom, here's a picture of me, I drew it just for you." They laughed over the Valentine cookie event at school, the prom dress incident, and shuddered at the thought of her first encounter with sex, and the way she treated it as just something that everyone experiences as a teenager. They reminisced about their meeting and how gloriously happy they have been all these years.

Some nights they went to the Lodge for dinner and stayed until the musicians began playing, then danced until late in the evening, going home too tired even to make love.

Peggy had scheduled the crews of workmen to sand and polish the hardwood floors in the living room while they were gone. She promised that the furniture in that room and in the rest of the house wouldn't be covered with dust from sanding, and that the new area rug would be in place when they returned. The painters would repaint the walls in the downstairs rooms with an updated, brighter shade of paint, and the backsplash in the kitchen would be tiled with miniature blue and white glass tiles to coordinate with the white cabinets and give the room a nautical look. Jennie and Tom were anxious to see the restoration, but they wanted to stay at the lake until the work was completed. They recalled the complete restoration of their home almost twenty years ago when they ended up camping in the house with workmen constantly underfoot. They didn't want a repeat of that scenario.

When they returned from Gull Lake, they wandered through the house inspecting the area rug in tones of beige, blue and gold that gave a note of restful elegance to the living room, the freshly painted rooms with slightly bolder colors replacing the quiet placid tones of the past, the kitchen that seemed new with the blue and white recycled glass tile backsplash that added shimmer to the kitchen, and her freshly painted office. Peggy had suggested that Jennie select a new color scheme for the master bedroom, but Jennie told her she would wait until spring, she didn't feel like tearing it apart now. They had been busy with the wedding in Santa Barbara, the speaking engagement and book signing in Seattle, and then a week at Gull Lake where they were finally able to relax, but now she had to get back to her writing routine. Then, as an after thought, she realized that Thanksgiving was fast approaching. Charlie and Lisa would be coming for the weekend, and she would be busy with preparations.

"Peggy, we love everything you have done. Our home looks fresh and new. Your choice of colors is so tasteful and beautiful."

"I'm glad you like everything. Your selection of colors for the area rug is perfect. The room needed color and texture."

"You made the right decision to go into interior design. I know you'll have a wonderful future, and we'll have a resident designer." Then she added, "How are things with you now, Peggy? Is everything okay?" She wondered if she had recovered from Steve's death, and at this point Tom entered the room, and he was anxious to hear her reply.

"I'm okay. I broke up with Ben. I realized that I liked being with him just because he was Steve's friend. I thought he would replace Steve, but he can't replace Steve, and we didn't have anything else in common. I think he felt the same way."

"You did the right thing. If you have doubts, it just wasn't meant to be." Jennie replied, and Tom told her she made the right decision, that she was vulnerable and not able to make a decision of the heart at this time.

"Now, I'm totally engrossed in an assignment for a new client. She came into the shop last week when I was there alone, and she began telling me about her home in Lake Forest that hadn't been updated or repainted in years. She said she was tired of its worn and tattered furniture. Now that her son is back home living with her she had a reason to redecorate and entertain again. She had been depressed living alone with no one to talk to and having no one who cared about her. She felt there was no need to have a pretty home if she was the only person there."

"At first, I thought she just wanted someone to talk to, but she asked me to come to her home and give her an evaluation and estimate on what needed to be done. I went there the following day, and she has a lovely old home that needs almost everything. I could tell it was a stately old home where in its early years entertaining took place on a grand scale. Even the grounds had been neglected. She gave me the impression that cost wasn't an issue, and it was obvious that she was a person of means. We walked through the downstairs rooms, and I gave her some recommendations of what should be replaced and what could be altered such as upholstering, etc. She liked my ideas and asked me to put in writing a proposal with cost estimates. I have been working on it, getting fabric and paint samples, etc. and will call her for an appointment when I'm finished."

"Peggy, that sounds like a wonderful opportunity for you. There aren't many people who can decorate without cost restraints. What is she like and what is her age?"

"She's very nice, a widow about 70 years old. She appears to be in good health, and she's attractive, too. Her aged face still reflects the beautiful girl she once had been. She said her husband was in the manufacturing business. Her son has taken over the business, and since he is in the process of getting a divorce, he moved back home. Her name is Elizabeth Burnham. I like her, and I'm really looking forward to working with her.

She said I should call her Beth since all her friends call her Beth."

"I'm sure you are looking forward to working with her, and I'm anxious to hear more about your project and her home. Suzanne is from Lake Forest, I wonder if she knows of the family. I'll ask her."

Tom told her she was involved in a very interesting situation, and he wanted to hear all about it.

A week later when Peggy had amassed a collection of sample books, fabric swatches, carpet samples, paint chips, and tiles, she called Mrs. Burnham for an appointment. The phone was answered by a woman who identified herself as her maid, and Peggy was relieved to know she had live-in domestic help and did not spend all day and night alone.

Driving up, she thought the home had the appearance of a chateau in France, yet it was not out of place on the North Shore of Chicago. Someone had once lavished love on it, and she was anxious to see the inside. Beth greeted her at the door wearing a beautiful bright blue knit dress. She had meticulously applied makeup and her silver hair was brushed back into a chignon at the nape of her neck. She had an aristocratic bearing which she had no doubt cultivated as a member of the North Shore's high society. She was bubbling with excitement and was eager to delve into Peggy's large tote bags.

"Beth, you look so pretty," Peggy remarked.

"Since I'm anxious to give this old house a complete makeover, I thought I could use a makeover, too. Please come in, dear, and show me what you brought."

She led her through the parquet-floored entry to the dining room where the samples and layouts of the rooms could be spread out on the long table as Peggy described in detail the extensive alterations she recommended. Beth was engrossed with every detail, and she spent a considerable amount of time asking questions and studying each item.

"This is becoming so tiring, I think we need to take a break. I'll ask Muriel to make some tea or would you prefer coffee?"

"Yes, let's take a break. Tea is fine. I think I have overwhelmed you with too many decisions."

Beth ushered Peggy into the living room, and Muriel, who she learned was her live-in maid, brought in a tray of tea and cookies and little cakes.

Beth asked Peggy if she could keep the samples and layouts a few days so that her son, Jeff, could approve them since he has moved back home to live indefinitely. "I want him to like everything as he will have to live with everything longer than I will. Martin and I lived her since we were married, and I hope Jeff will always want to live here."

Peggy assured her she could keep everything and she offered to return and meet with her son, if she liked.

"How long has your husband been gone?" Peggy asked.

"He died ten years ago, and I lost interest in everything; that's why everything looks faded and worn. Now I realize I was wrong. I still have a life to live, and I should live it happily and with a purpose. I want to get back to my charities and clubs and entertain again like we used to. So you see, the house needs some work."

"Your home will be beautiful. I will make certain everything is done to your desired perfection."

Peggy told her she knew how she felt and what she had been going through losing her husband. "I lost someone too, I know what you went through."

"Dear, I'm sorry to hear that, you are so young to experience the loss of a loved one."

Peggy blushed, "Yes, we were young and in love, and it hurt. He was killed when a deer ran into his car. It was so unexpected. I didn't think I could go on, but we all do."

"Yes, we both lost the person we loved the most."

Later, when Peggy was ready to leave, Beth said, "You indicated you could come back and go over everything with Jeff, would you join us for dinner sometime soon?"

Peggy said she would like that and told her she was free almost any night. Beth told her she would discuss it with Jeff tonight and call her tomorrow.

At dinner that night, Peggy related the day's events to her mother and father. They listened intently as she told them about the planned dinner and get-together with her son, Jeff, but they refrained from making any comments.

The next morning Beth called and asked Peggy if she could come for dinner that evening as Jeff had to leave the following day on a business trip, and he would be gone for a week. "Can you come at 6?" she asked.

"Yes, that would be fine; I'll see you at 6."

"Lovely meeting you," Jeff said in his best corporate manner as he opened the door wide. He was smiling in an approving way, as if he was pleased with Peggy's appearance. He looked to be in his early thirties, his brown hair was cut short, his eyes were extremely dark, and his mannerism exuded confidence and power. He was about 6 feet tall, but his slimness made him appear taller. He was wearing a long-sleeve button-down shirt and well-pressed and creased chinos. It was evident he had been educated in the East at an Ivy League school.

"Come this way, mother is waiting. I understand that you are going to bring this old house back to life again. She is very impressed with what you are proposing to do, so I'm certain it'll be splendid."

During dinner, Jeff took the opportunity to learn more about Peggy. "Do you live in the Chicago area?"

"Yes, I live with my father and mother in Lincoln Park. We live in an old limestone duplex that we converted back to its former one-owner residence. We love our home and the neighborhood."

He continued the questioning, asking her how long she had been decorating, did she have any brothers or sisters, and what did her father do for a living. She told him that she graduated from the Architecture & Design School at the University of Illinois and then took a job with Levine Interiors, the leading interior design firm in Chicago. Beth pointed out that they have a great following on the North Shore. Peggy told him about her brother who was a professor at Columbia University in New York, that her father was a retired economics professor, and that her mother was a best-selling author. Beth spoke up and asked what she wrote.

Peggy told them her author's name was Jennie Rogers, and her most acclaimed book was A Brief Wondrous Life."

"Oh, I read that book and liked it very much," Beth replied. Jeff raised his eyebrows in astonishment as if he was truly amazed at her family and her own self-assurance.

After dinner, they proceeded to the study where Peggy showed Jeff the layouts and samples. She had meticulously drawn each room, then written in its dimensions, the measurements of the windows, and sketched in the tentative furniture placement. Then she had stapled in the color and fabric samples she was going to use in each room. She explained that all fabrics and trimmings would be ordered through vendors in the Merchandise Mart and their own seamstresses would be making all the draperies and slipcovers. Our talented staff takes pride in their workmanship.

"There's just one change I'd like to make, and that concerns the color scheme in the conservatory," Jeff said. "The pink floral fabrics on the chairs and the solid pink on the chaises are too overpowering. I'd prefer a green floral and solid green color."

"Your mother selected those fabrics," Peggy remarked.

"Well, I think the pink is too feminine, and it has to go. I'll talk to mother."

"Those fabrics do come in a beautiful moss green shade. My sample book is in the car, I'll go get it."

"Would you please, then I think we can wrap this up."

Peggy went to the car and retrieved her sample book, and as she was nearing the study she overheard Jeff telling his mother, "she knows her job and has good taste, but I'd rather have green as the primary color in the observatory."

Peggy didn't hear his mother's reply as she didn't want it to appear that she had been eavesdropping. They both approved the moss green color, and as Peggy was packing up her materials and preparing to leave, Jeff told her he liked what she proposed to do and asked if she would be there often to oversee the workmanship. She assured him she would oversee the project to its conclusion. She didn't seem to be at all intimidated by him.

Obviously pleased, he said, "Well, with the amount of work to be done around here, we'll be seeing a lot of you."

Peggy smiled and said she looked forward to working with them.

Chapter Fifteen

November mornings were frosty, and darkness set in earlier in the evening. The trees had shed their leaves, and the lake breezes had become predictably cooler. Jennie and Tom were becoming accustomed to their semi-idleness, and each morning they started the day with a walk to the lake. The Thanksgiving weekend was a week away, and Charlie and Lisa would be spending the long weekend with them. They discussed their plans as they walked.

Tom picked up Charlie and Lisa at the airport, and the weekend promised to be a series of laughs and surprises. Lisa surprised Jennie and Tom when she playfully lifted her tunic top to reveal her slightly round, protruding belly, announcing, "We are going to have a baby in May." Charlie told them they needn't bother counting months. "Yes, Lisa was a month pregnant on their wedding day." He rubbed his hand over her belly and announced, "Here is your first grandchild!"

Jennie and Tom were elated and the four of them stood together hugging each other and laughing.

Thinking back to her own pregnancies, Jennie asked Lisa if she was going to have the gender test, and they said they preferred to be surprised. However, Charlie said he hoped it would be a boy and, of course, Lisa hoped for a girl.

Peggy arrived at home from work just as dinner was being served, and the dinner conversation revolved around her. Since she was the youngest and only single member of the family, naturally her love life became the topic of light-hearted conversation. Lisa asked if she had a boyfriend.

"I don't have a boy friend now; I've been very busy with a huge interior design project for a lady and her son in Lake Forest. I'll be spending a lot of time there."

Both Charlie and Lisa questioned her about the project. Peggy told them about Beth Burnham, their gracious home, and her son, Jeff, who had recently moved back home. The entire project had to have his approval.

"What is he like?" Lisa asked.

"Nice looks, nice voice, nice manners," Peggy said.

"Is that it? Isn't there anything about him that would make him stand out from all the other guys on the North Shore?"

"He's handsome, he's an egotist."

"In other words, he's like all the other guys."

Peggy smiled and changed the subject. "Is it true that you are pregnant, Lisa?"

"Yes, I'm due in May."

"Are you going to retire and become a full time mom?" Peggy asked.

"Oh, no, I'll have a three-month maternity leave and then go back to work. Of course, I'll be working at home during those three months. Charlie wanted me to quit working and be a stay at home mom, but my work means so much to me. Its what I strived to do for so many years, and now that I've reached my goal in life, I couldn't just toss it aside and stay home doing housework and raising children. We are in the process of interviewing nannies. I won't be the housewife sitting at home waiting in an apron to hear all about her husband's day. I'll go to soccer games and school plays, but I need my job, my outlet in life."

Jennie was startled at their conversation. She had raised her own children and wouldn't have considered leaving them in the care of a stranger. *They don't need the money, Lisa could easily retire. She doesn't know what she will be denying herself. Kids today don't know or understand the values of being a parent. She was tempted to tell them so, but if she did, it would only drive a wedge between them, and she certainly didn't want to be the proverbial mother-in-law who was a constant interference in their lives.* She looked at Tom to see his reaction, and he had a look that said "don't go there, it's out of our hands." She nodded and thought, *well, I'm certain everything will be just fine.*

While they were enjoying dessert, Jennie said, "I almost forgot to tell you that we asked Roger Smith to join us for Thanksgiving dinner. Charlie, you remember our trips to Quincy to visit Lynn and Roger, don't you? You know that Lynn died, and since Roger is alone, we thought it would be nice to share the holiday with him. Well, we were shocked when he asked if it would be all right if he brought his lady friend with him. Naturally, we told him, yes, please do. We are anxious to meet her."

"We should all be happy that Roger found someone to share the rest of his life," Tom said.

"I agree, Dad, I'm glad you invited him. It will be good to see Roger again," Charlie remarked.

Roger and his friend, Susan Thomas, arrived shortly before noon. Susan was a kindly-looking woman with her graying blonde hair turned under in a pageboy. She was wearing an emerald green dress, and she wore an emerald necklace. She was somewhat overdressed, but she was self-confident so she didn't appear out of place. Roger was wearing his best suit and tie, and they were a nice-looking couple who would age well together. After introductions, Roger joined Jennie in the kitchen for a private conversation. He knew she would want to know how he had coped with Lynn's death.

"How are you doing, Roger? How have you managed after Lynn's death?

"The grief was devastating; there were days when I didn't think I could go on. There were times I didn't have the energy or desire to prepare a meal, and I'd think of driving to a restaurant, then I'd shake my head and go back into the house and listen to the silence. Some mornings when I awoke in the dark, I'd run my hand over the cool sheet beside me expecting Lynn to be there. I felt so isolated, alone. Then you think. There's so much unsaid in a marriage because we think there will be plenty of time, other occasions. Then the guilt began. That's the worst. But I've gotten past that now that I have Susan in my life."

"I hired Susan to manage the office, and she was the first and only person I interviewed. When I learned she had insurance experience, I knew she could replace Lynn – in the office, that is. Gradually, we became close friends and discovered we needed each other. She had lost her husband shortly before Lynn passed away, and we commiserated together. We've discussed marriage, but haven't set a date. You two will be the first to know."

"That's wonderful news, Roger. You need her and she needs you. You belong together. We are so happy for you. Now let's join the others before Susan wonders if you have deserted her."

The aroma of the turkey and dressing was so tempting they didn't want to wait another moment. Tom said, "I'll carve the turkey," and everyone gravitated to the kitchen. Jennie made the gravy, Peggy mashed the potatoes, and Lisa dished up the dressing and vegetables. Charlie poured the wine, and Susan filled the water glasses. Tom said grace, and the commotion of dishes passing back and forth began. Soon they were saying "more gravy, please," as they asked for seconds. Some said "I shouldn't" to offers of seconds or thirds, and then took some anyway. There was a comment that this year the turkey was the best ever, which led to a discussion of the different ways of preparing the bird. But, of course, they would probably continue preparing it as they always had year after year. Jennie knew Thanksgiving would become her favorite holiday because everyone would be coming home.

*****

Chapter Sixteen

Jennie centered a vase of lilies and gerbera daisies on the kitchen table. Then she opened a bottle of red wine and brought out the glasses with the full, round bodies, rye crackers, and some Brie and Danish Havarti cheese.

Suzanne was coming over to tell her all about Lauren's engagement party. She had only been home from Africa for a month, and already she and Peter Adler had announced their engagement. The last time Jennie saw Peter was at Lauren's bat mitzvah. He was a tall, gangly kid with a full-blown case of acne, and now he was the tall, charming and handsome heart doctor, Peter Adler.

"We were surprised to hear that Lauren and Peter were engaged. We thought that relationship ended long ago."

"Matt and I were a little surprised too. They corresponded while she was in Africa and while he was in college and medical school – that was ten years, so it shouldn't have been surprising. We like Peter a lot, we're very happy for them."

"Will there be a wedding soon?" Jennie asked.

"We hope so. We want to have grandchildren. I hope they don't wait so long that Lauren will have problems getting pregnant. She's 32 years old now. Or, I hope she doesn't get so wrapped up with her work, that she doesn't have time for children. Now that she's taking over the business, we can't get her away from that plant."

"Even if she does have conception troubles, there's always adoption. There are lots of babies in the world who need good homes."

"That's true, but we want to have our own grandchildren; children of our genetic expression. I want Lauren and Peter to be happily married with a family of their own. Every parent wants grandchildren."

"Incidentally, Lisa's expecting, I'm going to be a grandmother," Jennie glumly stated.

"That's wonderful, why are you so despondent?" Suzanne replied. "Think of the fun you'll have and the frequent trips to New York to see the baby."

Jennie picked up her wine glass and quickly set it down. "I know what you're saying, and really both Tom and I are thrilled and can hardly wait for our first grandchild. It's just that I feel so depressed. I see a fat, graying woman with wrinkled skin, age spots and protruding veins. You know, the dour grandmotherly type, and I'm not ready for that. I wonder if I should be taking Prozac or Xanax. Sometimes I just don't feel like myself, and I don't know what to do about it."

"You a wrinkled, gray grandmother? You have it all wrong, that's not how I see you at any time."

"I'm already getting fat. Look at my stomach," and she lifted her T-shirt and unbuttoned her jeans. "Just look at how fat I am, and I've noticed several gray hairs, especially at my temples."

"Well, I have my share of gray hairs, and your stomach isn't any bigger than mine, and she lifted her T-shirt and unbuttoned her pants to show her small protruding belly. We all get a tummy with age." Her red hair was pulled back in a pony tail, and Jennie didn't see any gray hairs. "Jen, you're only as old as you feel. Remember, youth is not a time of life, it is a state of mind."

Tom walked into the kitchen and abruptly stopped. He could not disguise a look of shock, "What is this? Should I leave?"

They burst out laughing at the look on his face and the humor of the situation. He joined them for a glass of wine, and Jennie told him they were talking about grandmothers and growing old and fat.

"You aren't fat, I like you just the way you are," Tom replied.

"But do I look old?"

"Not a day over thirty."

"You lie, but I like to hear it."

"I read in one of your magazines that fifty is the new thirty, which means you are actually just thirty-four," Tom said.

"Trust me when I tell you fifty-four is not the new thirty-four," Jennie replied.

Suzanne asked, "When is Lisa due?"

"In May, and Tom and I plan to be there. Lisa will need some help, and we want to see the baby right away. We don't know whether it will be a boy or girl; they want to be surprised. Of course, Charlie wants a boy and Lisa wants a girl. We'll stay for a week and then leave them alone as a family."

****

The day that they were scheduled to leave for Christmas with Charlie and Lisa, snow had begun falling in New York around eight that morning and by early afternoon seven inches had accumulated, with another six inches forecast. Their flight was cancelled.

O'Hare was bedlam with stranded travelers urgently needing to get to New York for Christmas. Tom and Jennie rescheduled their flight to arrive New Year's Eve. The opening of Christmas presents would have to wait.

When they arrived at four in the afternoon, the sky in New York was dark, but the colored Christmas lights on the quince outside the living room window shone brightly framing the large lighted Christmas tree inside. A fire was burning in the fireplace. It was December 31st, but for them it was Christmas Eve. They lit candles, laid out plates on a buffet table in the dining room, put on some Christmas records, and helped themselves to a delicious beef tenderloin dinner. They counted the months and days until Lisa was due and they would become grandparents.

****

"You're very perceptive, I like that," Jeff exclaimed.

Peggy was putting the finishing touches on the observatory, and she remarked, "I've been thinking that we should replace the brick patio surrounding it with a lush bluestone tile courtyard. It would better anchor the observatory to the backyard, and I would like to see it softened with a green-and-white themed garden surrounding the courtyard. We could plant camellias, a tea olive hedge, various hostas, hydrangeas and ferns. Here are some pictures of a similar garden that we did for another client."

"Oh, that's beautiful," Beth gushed. She looked at Jeff and said, "Let's go ahead with Peggy's plan. The backyard needs a lot of work, and those old bricks in the patio have either broken or they have sunk into the ground. It's so uneven, it's dangerous."

"You're right, mother, those bricks need to be replaced. I like the appearance of bluestone tiles, and the surrounding hedge and garden will give us privacy. I like it so much I'm not going to quibble over the cost," and he winked at Peggy.

"Bluestone tiles are more costly than brick, but the entire project won't be as expensive as you might think. I'll work up the cost and have a figure for you tomorrow."

"What about flowers?" Beth asked.

"You could have several potted plants with pink and white flowers in the courtyard."

"Oh, that sounds lovely," Beth replied.

As Jeff was seeing Peggy to the door, he remarked, "I really like what you are doing for mother, and she approves of everything you propose. You two work well together."

"It's easy to please your mother, she has exquisite taste. I'll see you tomorrow."

Chapter Seventeen

A green sign, "CAPE COD, Next Exit," flashed by, and Charlie relaxed. He had been sitting in traffic jams for hours. The radio announcer warned, "Everyone's headed back to the Cape!" As summer approached, an exodus of people came from Boston and New York to spend weekends or vacations at the Cape. Tourists smeared their bodies with tanning lotion and absorbed more sun than was healthy. They collected the beach glass like it was diamonds instead of chipped pieces of soft drink bottles. A car honked, and Charlie merged into another lane. He and Lisa would go together to the Cape in another month after the baby was born. They'd slather on sun block and swim in the ocean and eat enough fresh seafood to grow gills. Charlie was finished with school, and he came to open the house and do some cleaning to ready it for their summer vacation. Lisa would have joined him, but she was due in two weeks, and she was so big she would have been uncomfortable riding in the car for a long length of time.

He drove through the hilly countryside dotted with ponds, streams and bogs, past the ever-present salt marshes toward Millway Beach. As he drove up the road next to the ocean, he squinted at the sky hoping the fog would lift. There were rays of sun shooting through the breaks in the clouds, so it was promising. He would open all the windows and air out the house, and then go from room to room cleaning the windows and floors and dusting the furniture. He wanted the house to be ready for Lisa and the baby. She had a three-month maternity leave before going back to work, and they wanted to spend those three months at the Cape. Their baby would spend its first three months of life on Cape Cod.

As he was finishing up, the sun was shining brightly and the ocean breezes cooled the house and cleared the musty smell from the rooms. His stomach growled from hunger, and he decided to drive into town for an order of fried oysters from the Oyster House. As he was about to leave, the phone rang. He wasn't expecting any calls and he felt a wave of panic as he snatched the phone from the receiver. The woman's voice calmly stated she was calling from New York Presbyterian Hospital, and his wife had arrived and was going through labor. She had asked the nurse to please call you as soon as possible.

Charlie gulped and told the woman he was on his way. First, he had to find a station and fill up with gas. While at the station, he picked up some candy bars to stave off his hunger and then he pulled out on Interstate 95 heading for New York. It would be a four hour drive, and as he observed the bumper to bumper traffic heading to the Cape, he felt fortunate to be traveling away from it to the city. The car didn't seem to be going fast enough, but he stayed at the speed limit. This was not the time to be stopped for speeding. The sun was setting, and he flicked on his lights. Would he get there in time? He had promised Lisa that he would be at her side in the delivery room. He then wondered if it would be a boy or a girl, and he was tempted to press down harder on the gas pedal, but changed his mind.

Suddenly lights flashed in the rearview mirror; evidently he had inadvertently pressed hard on the gas pedal. "Damn," he uttered and pulled off to the side of the road. The officer stepped next to the car and asked if he was in a hurry.

"Yes, Sir," Charlie said excitedly. "My wife is having a baby; she's at the hospital now."

"Well the baby's going to get here when its ready, and you want to get their safely, don't you?"

Charlie sheepishly said, "Yes, Sir."

"Okay, go ahead and take it easy."

Charlie breathed a sigh of relief and realized his palms were sweating. He unwrapped a candy bar and chewed on it to relax. He thought of the baby, his son, being born. He would be a healthy baby, they would all go home, and this would be a story they'd laugh about later.

Finally, he reached the hospital. It was bright and noisy, and he walked down the hallway to snag a nurse to ask, where are they? But every time he approached a nurse, she glided past him, her shoes whispery on the waxed tile as she hurried by. He headed for the main desk where a flurry of people had gathered. "Lisa Doyle," he said breathlessly.

The nurse looked up at him, "Oh, Mr. Doyle, she's in the delivery room," and she directed him to the elevator. "Third floor, take a right, the room number is 330."

He walked so fast he skidded on the black and white tiled floor. The elevator door opened, and he pressed the 3rd floor button. He turned to go right down the hall, and there was Room 330. Lisa was on an operating table with the doctor telling her to push, push. Charlie crouched beside her, holding her hand, watching the baby being born. When the doctor held her up and Charlie saw her small face with big eyes wide open and looking right at him, he began to cry.

"Why are you crying?" Lisa asked. "Is the baby all right?"

"Yes, she's beautiful," Charlie told her, wiping at his tears and kissing her.

Then the doctor told them they had a healthy baby girl, and the nurse took her away to get cleaned up.

When Charlie called his parents to tell them the news, Jennie answered the phone.

"You're a grandmother," Charlie burst out. All he heard was sobs, and he wondered why she was crying.

"Mom, don't cry, it's a girl, and she's beautiful."

Jennie was really happy, but Charlie's sudden outburst that she was a grandmother brought back thoughts of an aged and gray-haired woman. She collected her composure, and said, “Charlie, that’s wonderful, how is Lisa?”

“She’s fine, a little tired, so she’s sleeping now. She’ll be going home day after tomorrow, and then a few days later, we are going to the Cape. We want you and Dad to come to the Cape for a week or two.”

“Charlie, that sounds wonderful; we’re anxious to see the baby. What’s her name?”

“We decided to name her Sara, Sara Jane Doyle, and she looks like a Sara. She has a cute little face with big blue eyes.”

“That’s a pretty name, I like it a lot. Tom’s out cycling, I can hardly wait to tell him.”

The next morning, Charlie rode the elevator up to the maternity ward. The walls were painted with brightly-colored murals of animals frolicking around the room. The staff all wore smocks with teddy bears on them and everyone was smiling. He rounded a corner and saw Lisa’s room. She had taken a shower and was eating breakfast before the nurse brought the baby in for nursing. He kissed her and told her he loved her.

"I saw her being born," Charlie said. "I heard her first cry."

"I know, I heard her first cry, too. Isn't it wonderful?"

Then a nurse came and took her finished breakfast tray away and returned with a tiny crimson-faced baby wrapped in a pink blanket. She looked clean and smelled of baby powder. Her brown hair was straight and long. She began to cry and Lisa brought her to her chest where she snuggled in and contentedly began nursing. She wasn't a particularly pretty baby, but she was healthy and whole, and her parents thought she was the most beautiful baby they had ever seen.

When Sara had finished nursing, she began to cry and Charlie took her into his arms. He knew that he would sacrifice his life for her. He talked softly to her saying, "I'll take care of you, Sara; I'll buy you a puppy, maybe a pony, I'll take you to the beach…" The baby continued to cry and a nurse came in and took her from Charlie's arms. "She needs changing, and then I'll put her down for a nap."

Two weeks later they were at the Cape, and Jennie and Tom arrived, honking the horn of their rental car, and then rapping on the screen door, their faces eagerly peering through the screen.

They hugged and Jennie asked, "Where is she?" Lisa told them she had just put her down for a nap, but quietly led them to the baby's room. Jennie and Tom beamed as they studied her sleeping face. "She's so pretty. I'm telling you, you're going to have to throw us out," Jennie whispered. Lisa told them she just loved staring at her thinking, "Where did you come from?" "How is it possible you are here with us?"

Charlie said, "Some fathers don't want to go into the delivery room, but I wanted to. I wanted to be with Lisa." Tom told them about Charlie's birth and how he stayed in the delivery room. He said he thought that experience helped fathers bond with their babies.

That evening Charlie grilled salmon, and Tom took charge of the salad while Lisa and Jennie fed Sara and got her ready for bed.

After dinner, Lisa scooped big scoops of vanilla ice cream into glass bowls and topped them with fresh, strawberries. The strawberries were grown on the Cape, and they were big and sweet.

The night was cooling down, and there were stars in the sky. "Come on, let's sit out on the front porch, and Charlie poured each of them a glass of white wine. Jennie picked up her glass and sipped. "This wine is heavenly." They sat and talked and watched the moonlight sparkling on the water. "We love the smell and sound of the ocean, the waves rushing to the shore, and the salt air, and we love the endless beaches, even the sand that always gets into everything, including the bed sheets," Lisa remarked.

Charlie commented, "The residents who have lived here for years hate the way the town fills up and empties out with the seasons. They also complain about the increased traffic and lack of parking space in town. They don't realize that the tourists spend a lot of money here, and traffic conditions are a trade-off. But, we love the character of the Cape and living on the ocean. We always knew we would end up here."

The following day they went into town and mingled with the summer people dressed in their touristy Cape Cod T-shirts. The scent of oven-fresh pastries and hot coffee drew them into the door of the most fabulous bakery. It was crowded with customers who had to take a number and wait to be called. The baked goods from scones, muffins, calzones, and homemade trail mix were well worth the wait. Jennie bought a T-shirt for Peggy, and they went into a baby's store named, "Beautiful Beginnings," and Jennie and Tom bought some cute outfits for Sara. They went to the Fudge Factory for fudge to munch on, they stopped at a farmer's stand and bought fresh-picked corn on the cob, and before they went home they stopped at the Crab Shack and bought some crab cakes for dinner. "We have a tendency to eat lots of seafood when we are here," Lisa said. "It's always available and fresh."

After dinner they ate cherry pie out on the patio, and they were talking and enjoying their coffee when the man and woman who lived next door walked over to ask about their new baby. Charlie invited them to sit down and enjoy some coffee with them. They were introduced as George and Ellen Anderson, and he was the editor of **Cape Cod Magazine**. After George learned that Jennie was an author, he asked if she would be interested in becoming a contributing writer to his magazine, explaining they would like to have a non-resident who would write with a different point of view to thereby create new interest in the magazine. In other words, get away from the same old perspective.

Jennie was surprised, but her eyes gave an indication of interest. "Currently, I'm in between books, and it would be a pleasant diversion from fiction. I love the Cape and writing from a first-time tourist's point of view might be something you would like?"

George said, "That's exactly what the magazine needs. It might encourage visitors and even long-time residents to become new subscribers. People tire of repetition and long to read something different and exciting. Would you please send me an article for approval. If I like it, we'll sign you on."

"Our magazine is a lifestyle magazine. We tell people where to find the best restaurants, beautiful homes, arts and culture, events, surfing, best clam chowder, everything there is to see and do up and down the Cape. Weddings are a big feature. You'd be surprised at the number of people who come here to be married. We only publish ten issues a year. There's not much to write about after the tourist season. It gets pretty quiet around here; many businesses close for the winter."

"Incidentally, Tom writes non-fiction. He also is a motivational speaker," Jennie added.

"Is that so," George replied, and he asked Tom for more information.

Tom told him about some of his previous assignments and told him that from here they were going to Wilmington, Delaware where he would speak at DuPont Company's annual sales meeting.

"That sounds like the perfect retirement job – you can be as busy as you want to be."

"Exactly, that's why I decided to go into public speaking. The travel is something we enjoy too."

"Well, I'm certainly glad I got to meet you folks, and I feel that we'll be seeing more of you."

"Yes, I hope so, I'll write an article soon and send it to you," Jennie replied.

Then Charlie and Lisa walked them into the house to see their sleeping daughter.

After Jennie and Tom left them, Charlie and Lisa continued to enjoy their vacation. They went to drive-in movies, and while Sara slept in the backseat, Charlie and Lisa held hands, stuffed themselves with popcorn, and watched double features. They went to the beach, spreading out soft blankets under a huge umbrella to protect Sara from the sun, and they became active and adoring parents. Lisa talked calmly to Sara while diapering her, telling her about books she was reading or what was on the news, and when Charlie teased her, she smiled. "It doesn't matter what you say," she told Charlie. "Babies just need to hear your voice." She sang to Sara while she was bathing her, and when she cried in the middle of the night, she was up and by her side before Charlie even reached for his robe."

Charlie felt left out as a father, and sometimes he insisted, "No, let me."

He would stand over the crib with Lisa, the two of them mesmerized by Sara, who did nothing but sleep, eat and wet diapers regularly.

"Does she look like me?" Charlie asked. "Do you think she has my eyes?"

Lisa laughed. "Don't be silly. She's the image of me."

Chapter Eighteen

When Jennie and Tom left the Cape, they returned to New York and went to LaGuardia Airport for their flight to Wilmington, Delaware for Tom's address at the DuPont sales meeting.

During the two-hour flight Jennie had time to gather her thoughts about an article in Cape Cod Magazine while Tom put the finishing touches to his speech. She had brought a copy of the magazine with her, and she was excited and eager to begin what she hoped would be a new career. For the past year she had felt worn out and wanted to slow down. She longed to do something new and different, and she felt the magazine was the perfect outlet to get her creative juices flowing again. They both loved the Cape, and they planned to return, so the magazine would be an incentive to stay active and involved in the lifestyle of the Cape. She even toyed with the idea of purchasing a summer home there. She flipped through the magazine looking for the real estate section. There it was, the most beautiful house she had ever seen. It was sided with white clapboard with dusty blue shutters, two stories high, and with a generous wraparound porch. She looked over at Tom; he had dozed off. It's just as well, she thought, now was not the time or place to talk about buying property on the Cape.

Tom's audience was the sales staff of the Biochemicals Division of DuPont. About 500 men and women had been flown in from their district offices in the United States and Canada for the meeting. Jennie and Tom received a tour of DuPont's headquarters in Wilmington, and they were very impressed with their facilities.

It was late at night when the cab pulled up in their driveway, and they both heaved a sigh of relief to be home. Even though they disliked having to leave Charlie and Lisa and the baby, it was good to be in their own home. Jennie walked through the house admiring the recent changes Peggy had made. This place would always be the home where they would long to return.

Jennie rose early the next morning even though she hadn't slept well from their travels. All night she thought about the article she would write for Cape Cod magazine, and she was anxious to put her thoughts on paper. She desperately wanted to be on the writing staff of a distinguished magazine, and so she wrote:

"In many respects a visit to Cape Cod today is a journey back some 300 years. Many people have worked long and hard to keep this area preserved as closely as it was originally. It is impressive to find the old buildings so well cared for. Certainly, when the town officials are concerned over whether an old church or building should have aluminum siding instead of the traditional narrow wood clap boards, it shows love and concern for the preservation of the history of the Cape.

Today, the natural landscape of Cape Cod is little changed. Large areas of forest, dune, beach, and marsh separate small villages. This unspoiled natural beauty makes Cape Cod a favorite vacation area."

*****

It was a beautiful day to work outside, and Peggy had come to supervise the planting of the hedges and other plants that would surround the bluestone tiled courtyard. Walking up the curved entrance to the front door, she paused to admire the summer flowers in full bloom.

Beth answered the door exclaiming with excitement, "You arrived just in time; the workmen are in back unloading all the shrubs and bushes."

"That's good," Peggy replied, "I'd like to get them in the ground today since rain is forecast tomorrow."

Over a lunch of soup and salad, Beth told Peggy that Jeff's divorce was to become final today, and he would probably be home early so she hoped everything would be planted. She wanted it to be a surprise as he was very anxious for the project to be completed.

"It will be a happy ending to a stressful day," she said.

The workmen were busy all afternoon, and about 4:30 they cleaned the dirt and debris from the courtyard and drove off. Peggy arranged the potted plants with pink and white flowers attractively around the courtyard and put the chaise lounges and chairs in their places and stood back to admire what she had created.

"It's beautiful, I love it," Jeff said as he burst from the door of the conservatory.

"Thank you. I think it turned out quite well, and I'm glad you think so," she replied.

He was in an exuberant mood, and he stated, "This calls for a drink."

Peggy knew he wasn't referring to the courtyard. He called for Muriel to bring some wine and cheese and crackers.

Jeff lifted his glass and joyfully stated, "The divorce is final!"

*****

Jennie was anxious to tell Suzanne all about their trip to the Cape and their first grandchild. It was a warm summer day, and they decided to meet at the beach. Tom and Matt would join them, and they would go to Lake Michigan's North Beach. It was within walking distance for both couples.

Jennie brought pictures of Sara and Charlie and Lisa. Suz and Matt thought Sara was adorable. Suz told them they might be grandparents soon as Lauren and Peter finally decided they would marry in the fall.

Jennie also broke the news that she was now a contributing writer for **Cape Cod Magazine.** She had submitted a story shortly after they returned home, and the editor accepted it and sent a contract.

"Does that mean you have given up writing fiction?" Matt asked.

"I don't know, Matt, I've been in a slump, feeling completely drained of creativity, so I decided to take some time off to see if I actually could go back to writing novels. There were times when I just wanted to call it quits and retire."

"You aren't alone, most authors experience dry periods. Usually some time off is all they need. Give it a try. You're a talented writer. I'd hate to see you give it up." Matt replied.

"I'll see how I feel when fall arrives and I no longer have to write for the magazine. I never thought I'd be writing for magazines, but it's rather enjoyable. I like doing the reporting. I like talking to people; I like the whole process, and I could make a decent living doing it."

"I know," Matt said. "There are many essayists who do it for a living. Nowadays, magazines pay a relatively good fee. But what about The Sequel, you aren't going to abandon that are you?"

"No, certainly not. Since it's my memoir, it will be a work in progress. I'll get back to it this winter. I actually feel the summer magazine assignment was just what I needed to get out of the slump I was in."

"Hey, do you sexy women want to go in the water?" Tom asked.

Both Jennie and Suzanne were well-endowed and were wearing bathing suits that showed a lot of cleavage. He added, "It's very difficult to avoid staring at the curve of your breasts. Let's go in and cool off."

"At my age, I don't mind if you stare, and I'm happy to hear someone say I'm sexy." Suz replied.

"Yes, even old men aren't blind. I agree with Tom, it's hard to not stare. Let's go in," Matt said.

They plunged into the surf and nose-dived through the breakers. When the water finally became too cold they returned to their blankets and shivered even though the sun was hot.

Matt said, "I remember when we were kids, we'd flop down on the sand and roll over and over until we were covered with sand. Then as the sun heated our skin, the sand grains dried and could be brushed away. We called it 'breading.'"

"What was the purpose of that," Tom asked.

"No purpose, just a silly thing we liked to do."

Suzanne reached into her beach bag and drew out a deck of cards. "Let's dry off over a few hands of rummy."

*****

Peggy had just entered the shop of Levine Interiors when she heard the phone ringing. She was the first to arrive at work that day so she ran to take the call.

"Oh, I hope I'm not calling too early," Beth said.

"No, not at all. I ran an errand before opening up, so I'm a bit late. How are you, Beth?"

"I'm just fine. I've had second thoughts, and I've decided to replace the drapes in my bedroom. Even though I like them, I've lived with them too many years and now I want a change."

"Yes, I think you deserve a change. There are so many new and beautiful fabrics on the market now. Offhand, I can think of a Cowtan & Tout fabric that would be pretty. I can bring some samples for you to look at."

"That would be wonderful. Are you free to come for lunch today?"

"Yes, would eleven-thirty be all right?"

"Eleven-thirty is fine. I look forward to see you again," Beth stated.

While driving to Lake Forest, she thought about Beth and their relationship since the redecoration of her home. Beth had contacted her periodically for advice on furniture arrangements or for a new piece of art, anything that would bring them together. They had bonded and now enjoyed a pleasant relationship. Sometimes Peggy wondered if Beth was lonely and simply wanted her company in the disguise of a business project. A month ago, she had called Peggy to find the perfect painting for her new pale-blue dining room. She had taken Beth to an art gallery on Oak Street where she selected an expensive seascape painting much to Jeff's consternation.

"Mother, I'm not a hedge fund manager!"

At times Peggy wondered if Beth's assignments were conceived to bring her and Jeff together as he always "just happened" to show up on those occasions. But she didn't mind if there was a pretext to Beth's requests. She had become attracted to him, and she daydreamed and wondered what his kisses would be like and what their life would be like if they were married. She envisioned vacations at Cape Cod and cruises on the Mediterranean. She dreamed of him holding her closely, their warm bodies feeling the coolness of the sheets.

Business at the shop was slow during the summer months, so she welcomed her projects.

It was a typical August day – hot and humid without a breath of air. Even the trees that lined the driveway stood motionless as if to conserve energy. Beth greeted her with a hug, as usual.

"It's such a beautiful day, I told Muriel we would be served in the conservatory. Is that okay?" The conservatory was air-conditioned as was the rest of the house.

"Yes, Beth, that would be very nice. We should take advantage of these last days of summer," Peggy replied.

Over chicken salad sandwiches with green grapes, they eagerly brought each other up to date on their recent activities.

"Yesterday I did volunteer work for our local historical society. I enjoy it so much; it has become a form of recreation." Then she remarked, "Oh, here comes Jeff" as he entered the conservatory. He was dressed in jeans that were tattered at the knees and there were loose threads hanging from the pockets.

Beth commented, "Rags are no longer a sign of poverty, they are an emblem of style."

Peggy smiled and greeted Jeff.

"What are you ladies up to today?" he asked.

"Peggy brought some samples of fabric for my drapes. You are just in time to see them," Beth replied.

"I'll let you two make that decision. I have to go shopping for a few things for my trip to China. I leave tomorrow."

"That sounds exciting – is it for business or pleasure?" Peggy asked.

"It's a business trip, but I'm going to do some sight-seeing, too."

He had never discussed his business when Peggy was around, and she didn't want him to leave so she asked him about it.

"We make electrical switches, thermostats and relays. The family business that Dad started is Burnham Electrical Company in Chicago. I took over running it after he died. We specialize in manufacturing switches, sockets and distribution boxes, and we have an annual output value of $50 million."

"It would seem to be a very profitable business," Peggy said.

"It is, but it's a very competitive business. We have to constantly be on top of the industry. Right now, the Chinese are our biggest competitors."

"Aren't they in every business! They even compete in the fabric market."

"Yes, they're into everything and at a cheaper price."

"In our business, we find that the quality of their merchandise doesn't compare with US-made goods."

"That's true, but they are gearing up to change that. Mark my word, they will be a power to contend with," Jeff stated. He looked at his watch and told Peggy he enjoyed seeing her again.

"Well, I'm off to buy some new shirts."

"There's a small menswear shop next to our shop. They have nice things. My father has gotten some things there. It has a red door with shiny brass hardware. You can't miss it."

"I'll check it out sometime." He gave his mother a peck on the cheek and left.

*****

The day after Jeff left for China, a shocking story appeared in the newspapers and on the television news. Mrs. Jeffrey Burnham was found dead in her apartment by her cleaning lady. It appeared that she had died from an overdose of drugs. Because of the earlier publicity surrounding their messy divorce settlement and Jeff's sudden disappearance from the country, he immediately became implicated in her death. It seemed the media were anxious to prosecute him before investigations could take place. The newspapers and the television news anchors all drew their own conclusions and were ready to "put the noose around his neck." If he hadn't been a millionaire, it would have hardly made the news at all. People are often drawn to wealth and power, and the media was no exception.

It was necessary for Jeff to leave China immediately and return to Chicago to attend to his ex-wife and defend himself. Of course, his mother became very distraught over the deluge of publicity. Peggy tried to console her and convince her that Jeff had nothing to do with his ex-wife's death and the truth would soon be revealed to everyone. Even though Peggy hadn't known Jeff for a great length of time she knew he couldn't be involved in anyone's murder.

Wherever Jeff appeared people whispered behind his back, "Imagine killing your own wife, someone you're supposed to love. People are becoming more violent these days despite the ban on handguns. One only has to open the newspaper to see that. It's too easy to get guns; that's the problem. They say it's as easy as buying a package of cigarettes."

Peggy was worried and upset since she wasn't able to talk to Jeff and find out the truth. Jennie and Tom also became very distressed. Even though they had not met the Burnham's, they knew from Peggy's involvement they were fine people, and Jeff could not be guilty of murder.

Even Suzanne and Matt were concerned; Suzanne knew of the Burnham's from Lake Forest, and she knew Jeff was innocent.

They all somehow survived the ordeal and normalcy began to return to their lives when Jeff was cleared of all accusations. The publicity came to an end, and now Jeff had to pick up the pieces and continue on with life.

One day he walked into Levine Interiors carrying a bag from the menswear shop next door. He told Peggy he had gone to the shop at her suggestion and liked the lines of clothing that they carried. "It may become my favorite store."

It was closing time, and he asked her if she would join him for dinner. "I know a place nearby where we can talk and have a good dinner. I have a lot of explaining to do."

Peggy was anxious to have a heart to heart talk with him about his ex-wife and her death, so she told him she would love to join him for dinner.

After they ordered a drink, Jeff told her he would like to tell her about his marriage to Diane and the reason for their divorce.

"When we met it was love at first sight. She was kind, beautiful and fun to be with. We had good times. Two years later, she met some new people and she changed completely. I didn't realize at first that it was drugs that made her change. Later it became very apparent. Her personality had changed, and she was spending a lot of money. When I began questioning the amount of money she was going through, she started buying things with our credit cards and then selling the merchandise for whatever she could get for it to use for drugs. I'd get the bills and wonder where was this stuff she was buying. We tried several rehab programs, but she wasn't really interested in helping herself. She would say she wanted to stay clean, but then she'd go out and get more drugs. I'd find stashes all over the house. She hid it everywhere. The drugs drove a wedge between us, so we decided to split. I gave her a generous settlement and alimony, but later she said the alimony wasn't enough and had her attorney petition the court for more. That did it, I told her she wouldn't get a dime more if she continued with the drugs.. She told me she would go to rehab and stick with it this time, but, of course, she didn't. I think she was trying to overcome her addiction but she didn't realize that the drug she took for insomnia could be more lethal than the drugs she was addicted to."

"After a six-week investigation and the results of an autopsy, the coroner announced that Diane

Burnham died of "combined drug intoxication." Her death was ruled an accidental drug overdose of the sedative chloral hydrate which became lethal when combined with other prescription drugs found in her system, one of which was Valium."

"She had used chloral hydrate as a sleep aid for quite some time and evidently she had built up a tolerance to it so she was taking more than the prescribed amount. It was determined that she took about 3 tablespoons, whereas the normal dosage was between one and two teaspoons."

"A large jar of methadone was found in her refrigerator, however, the autopsy found only methadone in her bile which indicated it had been ingested 2-3 days prior to her death and was not a contributing factor. The corner indicated that since methadone was used in the treatment of heroin and morphine addiction, it did not contribute to her death."

"It just happened that her death took place the evening before I left for China. She knew nothing of my trip. Naturally, the authorities thought I had a part in it and then left the country. You know the rest, the dreadful publicity, and what I had to go through to prove my innocence. A lot of people thought I was a spoiled rich kid who thought he could get away with murder. There are probably some who still feel that way. I'd be walking down the street and they'd yell, "Hey, Rich Boy."

"It was rough – I had feelings of guilt for not being there to help her. Not only was I personally sorry and grieving for her terrible death, I had to look out for the business. I couldn't let our business suffer because of it. I wanted to contact you and explain, but I couldn't let you become implicated in any way. I'm happy that you stuck by me, Peggy. Your faith in me means everything.

When they left the restaurant, Jeff linked his arm through Peggy's, and they walked down the street to his car, not talking, just walking silently, together.

*****

Chapter Nineteen

It was November, and the leaves were losing their intensity; they were poised ready to drop, waiting for the wind to do its part. Jennie was making plans for Thanksgiving. It was her favorite time of the year, and Charlie, Lisa and Sara would again come from New York to be with them. Peggy asked, "Mom, would it be okay to invite Jeff and his mother for dinner?"

"Why of course, it would be wonderful to have them," she replied.

Jeff again departed for China to complete the business he was unable to conduct on his previous trip. He would be gone for ten days, returning just prior to Thanksgiving. When Peggy invited him to have Thanksgiving dinner with her family, her invitation was a pleasant surprise, and he thought, "She really does care for me."

A few days later when Tom was bringing in the mail, he was studying a postcard and without saying a word he handed it to Jennie. It was from China, and it simply read, "God, I miss you, Peggy."

"How many dates have they had?" he asked.

"She had dinner with him just once that I know of," Jennie replied.

"Evidently, he's been infatuated with her for a long time," Tom said.

"Yes, it sounds as though he is in love and will sweep her off her feet. This Thanksgiving will be interesting. Remember when Charlie brought Lisa home and what a surprise that was!"

"I remember it well, and Lisa is the best thing that happened to Charlie and to our family. I can't imagine him without her," Tom replied.

"Well, I'm glad Jeff is coming here for Thanksgiving, we need to know more about him."

Charlie and Lisa with little Sara arrived at O'Hare the evening before Thanksgiving Day, and, of course, Tom was there to meet them. Sara was sound asleep, and they said she had been sleeping since noon. "She does that all the time," Lisa said. "She sleeps all day and wants to play all night."

Recalling Peggy's schedule as a baby, Tom said, "You should break that habit now so you're not up all night. Believe me, I know."

Jennie greeted them with hugs and kisses and took Sara into her arms. "Charlie, she looks just like you at that age. Charlie looked at Lisa as if he was waiting for her to deny the similarity, but Lisa ignored Jennie's remark.

"She's been sleeping most of the day, so we're going to try to keep her awake until bedtime."

"That won't be difficult to do," Jennie said as she began to play with her.

Peggy entered the room and greeted them with hugs. "I'm glad you're here, I want you to meet someone. Remember the decorating project for the lady in Lake Forest? I've invited her and her son, Jeff, to join us for dinner tomorrow. They're really nice people, I know you'll like them."

"Is he the rich kid from the North Shore?" Charlie asked.

"They have money, but they're practical, just like a lot of other people."

"Just kidding, seriously I'm looking forward to meeting them and giving my approval or disapproval. I have to look out for my kid sister." Charlie remarked.

"I'm sure you will like them," Peggy remarked.

Charlie liked to tease his sister about her boy friends. "I suppose he's handsome in the way all wealthy guys are handsome. Basic good looks with an air of confidence."

Peggy felt her cheeks flush and said, "Yes, he's handsome."

*****

When Jeff and his mother arrived for dinner it was as if they were extended family members returning once again to be a part of the annual Thanksgiving celebration. They had the appearance of a family that typically went for a walk after dinner and then played Scrabble in front of the fire long into the evening. Beth was genuinely pleased to meet Jennie and Tom, and Jeff and Charlie were the separated brothers who were reunited once again for food and football.

Jeff was dressed in black slacks and a black pullover sweater over a white button-down oxford shirt that went well with his dark penetrating eyes. Peggy was also wearing black pants with a black turtleneck sweater, and she and Jeff made an attractive couple.

Little Sara was fascinated with her sudden new audience, and she immediately became an entertaining little sprite much to everyone's enjoyment.

"She's never acted like this in front of strangers before," Lisa remarked. "Usually, she's quiet and inquisitive as she sizes up people. It's as if she knows you are special guests."

When Tom excused himself to check on the turkey, Beth said that her husband, Martin, also cooked their Thanksgiving turkey. "Men are much better cooks when it comes to turkey."

"I totally agree," Jennie said. "They have no trepidation at all. The size of the bird is more than I care to get involved with. I much prefer to take charge of the side dishes."

When Tom announced that the turkey was done, everyone moved to the kitchen to help get the food on the table." Soon everyone was seated and the commotion of dishes passing back and forth replaced conversation.

There was the usual sprinkling of "Do you remember when…" which caused everyone to comment on previous Thanksgivings, but they all concluded that this was the best Thanksgiving ever.

After dinner, Peggy helped clear the table and poured coffee for everyone. Jeff seemed to like seeing this domestic side of her.

While eating dessert the conversation turned to Jeff and his business. He told everyone that he also dabbled in real estate, that he owned a high-rise apartment building on the lakefront. Jeff went on to tell them the tenants in the penthouse apartment were moving to Florida to retire. "They've lived there for almost twenty years, so it needs a lot of work to bring it up to today's standards."

Peggy was surprised as neither he nor his mother had mentioned the apartment building previously. She and Beth had spent so much time together she thought she knew them well. She was hurt that she hadn't been told, and suddenly she felt they were strangers.

Jeff glanced at Peggy and saw the hurt, confused look on her face. "Peggy, would you like to go for a walk and wear off some of those delicious calories?" Then he rose and helped her from her chair. Peggy didn't resist; she wanted to hear what he had to say. When they were in the foyer and Jeff was helping her with her coat, he put his arms around her and held her close.

"Peggy, I would never knowingly hurt you," he murmured as he kissed a tear from her eye. Then he whispered, "I love you so much, Peggy."

While Jeff and Peggy were leaving, Beth continued the conversation stating that Martin and his brother, Joe, bought the apartment building as an investment. When Joe died, Martin bought his wife's share of the investment. When Martin died, it became Jeff's responsibility, and he and Diane moved into one of the apartments when they married. With the manufacturing business, it became too large a responsibility for Jeff so he hired a management company to manage it. Now there are two vacant apartments that need to be redecorated, and Jeff was going to ask Peggy and Levine Interiors to do the work. Because of Diane's death and the business trips to China, he hadn't had an opportunity to discuss it with Peggy yet.

The day was blustery and cold, but Jeff and Peggy decided to walk to the lake. They were oblivious to the weather; they just wanted to be together. There was so much they wanted to say to each other that they talked continuously. Occasionally, they stopped to hug to stay warm.

"If I could write a description of my fantasy woman, you'd be it."

"I'm not perfect, I'm not June Cleaver." Peggy replied.

"I don't want June Cleaver, I want Peggy Doyle, and to me you are perfect. I know that together we could have a wonderful life."

"And what do you think makes a wonderful life?"

"Security, travel, nice food, good manners, ambition, good health..."

"I think you have it all now, but you left out fun."

"Fun? Yes, there definitely should be a lot of fun and no more sadness than is absolutely necessary."

"That's the kind of life I want, too," Peggy said.

He cupped his hands on either side of her face and leaned down, pressing his lips against hers. The kiss was soft, slow, and sensual. There was no rush; it was just two people sharing the first of many kisses to come.

When Peggy and Jeff returned from their walk, their cheeks were flushed from the cold, their eyes were sparkling, and they were laughing. Jennie looked at Tom, and he smiled and nodded. Peggy hadn't looked this happy in a long time.

*****

At breakfast, Peggy announced that she would begin work on the penthouse right away because that was where she and Jeff would soon be living.

"Oh, do you have marriage plans?" Jennie asked.

"No, he hasn't actually proposed, but we have our future planned. We both like the same things, and we know what we want in life."

I'm glad to hear that both of you are in agreement," Tom replied.

Jeff's going to pick me up at 10, and we'll inspect the apartment to see what needs to be done. I'm anxious to see it and get started. We want our home to reflect both our tastes. We are both Francophiles, so everything will be very French in style. Jeff has some antiques and art that he picked up in France so we'll work around them."

"I remember not long ago you told us you had no interest in getting married and you were going to save money to go to Paris and live for a year."

"Yes, I remember saying that." Blushing, she said, "That was before I met Jeff."

The doorbell rang and Peggy went to the door.

"Good morning, you look wonderful," Jeff said. His eyes said it even before his words did. It was easy to see how much he loved her. The Friday after Thanksgiving was a holiday for them, and they wanted to spend the day together.

When they were seated in his car he turned to her and said, "Yesterday we talked about the material things we wanted in life, but what I really want is to spend the rest of my life with you. Will you marry me, Peggy?"

"Yes, Jeff."

He slid the single solitaire diamond ring on her finger. It fit perfectly. Then he pulled her close and kissed her tenderly. "I love you so much."

Looking into his eyes, she said, "I love you, Jeff, you make me very happy."

He was a very nurturing person, and she liked that about him. She loved his tenderness and the way he made her feel loved. He had brought fresh excitement into her life, a feeling she hadn't experienced in a long time.

"Now, let's go and take a look at our new home."

As they stood and looked out the floor to ceiling windows, Peggy was spellbound by the views of Lake Michigan and the City skyline. They were on the 24th floor, and the scenery was breathtaking. They carefully inspected each room, and Peggy jotted down everything that needed repair or replacement. When they came to the master bath, Jeff uttered, "Ugh, everything has to go!" The tile, as well as all the fixtures, was pink. Peggy agreed. "That's really out-dated, we will have to gut the entire room. We'll want a new shower and a Jacuzzi tub. We should have dual sinks, too, so we don't get in each other's way."

Jeff wanted to make the fourth bedroom into an exercise room. He liked to work out often, and he didn't want to spend the time in a gym. Peggy was in complete agreement; they would exercise together.

He saved the best to last, and when he took her out on their private terrace, they decided to order pizza and have lunch in the sun overlooking the lake.

After lunch they went back to work. Peggy asked if it would be okay to gut the kitchen and put in new cabinets, granite countertops, and new appliances. "Absolutely, as long as we are spending the money, we want everything to be the way we want it."

When he took her home they stood outside the door hugging and kissing.

"I had a wonderful day," she whispered.

"So did I," he said. "This was the first day of the rest of our lives, and I can't wait for the next day. Sleep well, and I'll call you tomorrow."

At breakfast the following morning, Peggy held out her hand for Jennie and Tom to see. "Jeff proposed, so we'll be planning our wedding."

"Your ring is gorgeous, I'm so happy for you," Jennie said

"Well, I'm glad to hear he proposed marriage. We were worried that you'd just live together like so many young couples are doing today. Your mother and I are totally opposed to that trend," Tom said.

"I'd never do that. We love each other so naturally we want to be married."

"We should start planning your wedding, making arrangements at the church, reservations for the reception; they need to be made as soon as possible. When do you plan to be married?"

"It's going to take a long time to renovate the apartment, and we want it to be finished when we get married, so we're thinking maybe April or May. We'll get a better idea when we start the work and get availability and delivery dates."

Then she told them all about their penthouse apartment.

"The building has 24 floors, and it has 84 units. Our apartment has 4 bedrooms and 4 baths. The fourth bath is a guest bath off the foyer. It has a living room, dining room, and library. The kitchen is big, but everything is so old, looks like the 40's. The view is fantastic – it overlooks the lake, Lincoln

Park, and the City skyline, and we'll have our own private terrace. But, the apartment needs a lot of work; the bathrooms and kitchen will be gutted."

Jeff called, and asked her if she would join him for lunch with his mother. "I'd like you to be with me when I break the news of our engagement."

"Yes, I would like to be with you when we break the news. I want to see the expression on her face. I hope she'll be happy."

"She'll be overjoyed. She thinks the world of you. Sometimes I think she tried to get the two us together when you were working on the house."

"It's funny, I had that same feeling."

*****

Beth hugged Peggy and said, "I'm so happy you could join us for lunch. Muriel is going to make her specialty – chicken pot pies. You are in for a treat, come on in."

"Mother, we didn't just come for lunch. We wanted to tell you we are planning to get married. I proposed to Peggy yesterday."

"That's wonderful, I was hoping the two of you would get together." She drew them close and kissed them. "Now maybe I'll have some grandchildren!"

"You'll probably have a whole pack of them," Jeff replied.

"A boy and a girl," Peggy said.

They discussed their marriage plans and the renovation of the penthouse.

"Incidentally, Margaret has invited me to come to Fort Lauderdale for Christmas, and she wants me to stay for a month or so."

"That's great, mother, it will be good for you to get away from winter for awhile. Charlie and Lisa want us to spend Christmas with them at the Cape, so this will work out well. I didn't want to leave you here alone," Jeff replied.

"I'm happy to hear that, I felt guilty about deserting you."

*****

Jennie, Tom, Peggy and Jeff flew from O'Hare to Boston on the 23rd enroute to Cape Cod. They rented a car to make the two-hour drive to Charlie and Lisa's. It was late afternoon, and the weather was overcast. The radio announcer said the temperature was 52 degrees but dropping. When they were near Barnstable and the ocean they noticed the water was dark almost black, and the wind was roiling the water, creating white caps.

"Looks like a stormy sea," Tom commented.

"That probably happens often at this time of the year, don't you think?" Jennie asked.

"I don't know, but its something to see. I've never seen water like that."

"I hope the storm stays out in the sea," Peggy remarked.

Driving through a town along the way, they saw a restaurant that advertised, "The best clam chowder on the Cape."

"That sounds so good, why don't we stop and get enough for all of us to have for dinner tonight."

"I second that," Jeff chimed in. "Let's find out what real clam chowder tastes like."

"Sounds good to me," Tom said as he steered the car into the parking lot.

They all decided to stretch their legs and go into the restaurant. Tom placed the order and Jennie picked up several packets of small crackers. Peggy said, "Look, they have New York cheese cake for dessert." Jeff hailed the waitress and six cheese cakes were added to the order. He picked up the check and gave it to the cashier with a $100.00 bill.

The car crunched on the gravel as they drove up to Charlie and Lisa's, the wind was stronger and the temperature had dropped considerably. Then they saw the lighted Christmas tree in the window, and Charlie ran out to greet them and help them with their luggage. They piled their presents under the tree along with the rest of them. They knew this Christmas on the Cape would be special.

"We brought dinner; we couldn't resist a restaurant's claim to have the best clam chowder on the Cape," Tom said.

Charlie said, "We have had their chowder, and it's good, but Lisa is trying to outdo them, and hers is pretty good."

"It's not just good, it's great, I'll make it for you sometime," Lisa replied.

The sound of voices woke Sara, and they were interrupted by a wail from the bedroom. She had been napping and now she wanted to be a part of the family. Jennie went with Lisa to get her, and Sara immediately started gurgling and laughing when she saw Jennie. She played with her while Lisa was changing and dressing her.

"She has grown since we saw her a month ago."

"Yes, she has. I don't dare buy clothes that she can't wear immediately because she outgrows them before she wears them." She put Sara on the floor in the living room, and after momentarily studying each person she crawled toward the tree.

"Her first Christmas is having fun tearing presents open and trying to grab the ornaments from the tree. We have to watch her constantly."

"Well, she takes after her father, we had the same problem with him," Jennie said.

When everyone had made themselves at home, Charlie announced that they may have some unusual weather tonight as a storm was brewing at sea. "The weather man said it probably won't come ashore, but everyone should take precautions just in case."

"What precautions?" Peggy obviously was worried.

"Stay away from the beach, put away lawn furniture, stay indoors, just the usual stuff," Lisa replied. "We don't have any lawn furniture outside and we've been winterized since we aren't living here full time. Being so close to the ocean, we have to expect stormy weather."

"Hey, we are forgetting some very important family news. Peggy and Jeff are planning to be married in the spring. Our family is growing," Tom announced.

Peggy held out her left hand, and the diamond glistened from the sunlight coming in the window.

"What a beautiful diamond," Lisa gushed.

"That's great, Sis. I wholeheartedly approve. Jeff, welcome to the family," Charlie said

"Where are you going to be married? Tell me all about it," Lisa replied.

"We'll be married in Chicago, and we would like you and Charlie to stand up for us. We haven't made plans beyond that except that it will take place in April or May. That's as far as we've gotten."

"We would be honored to be your attendants," Lisa said.

The roar of the sea sounded louder than before, and they all went to the front windows. It was four-thirty and just starting to get dark, but there was still enough light to see the waves and the surf. The water was very dark, it appeared to be black, and the gale-force winds agitated the stormy ocean. The waves were ten or twelve feet high. When they rushed to the shore and crashed against the rocks, the foam ran up the sand and then it ran back as far as they could see. All the tracks on the beach were filled with water and seaweed from the sea. They could hear the frenzied cries of seagulls. When the high waves receded, they could see large pieces of wood and other debris left in its wake. Then it began to rain, and it pounded against the windows obstructing their view.

"Whew, I wouldn't want to be out there tonight!" Tom said.

Charlie and Lisa went to the kitchen and returned with a tray of appetizers and red and white wine.

Charlie picked up on Tom's comment about not being outside. "Soon the scavengers will be out there foraging for driftwood and anything of value that might have washed up on shore. Anything that they find belongs to them, and sometimes they find valuable things from wrecked ships. They can sell the driftwood for a pretty good sum of money, so it's a way of life for some people. We can't see them, but they're probably out there now. They have lived here all their lives, and they aren't afraid of the ocean storms, they want to be the first to pick up the debris. The beach will be strewn with debris from one end to the other. There's a sort of silent oath between the scavengers. The debris gets too heavy to carry with them for a distance so they stack their loot in piles as they go. When another scavenger sees a pile, he knows it belongs to someone else, and he moves on. It's the honor system."

"The ultimate beach bum!" Jeff replied.

"Those scavengers aren't young and strong; they're old men with bleached and weather-beaten faces, wearing weather-beaten coats and hats that have seen a lifetime of salt water. They have the face of an old man who is too grave to laugh and too tough to cry. It's serious business to them." Charlie said. "I hope all the fishing boats made it back to shore, there's nothing worse than a boat being late or lost and unable to make it home for Christmas."

"That's a part of the Cape I didn't know about. Jennie commented.

"Is anyone hungry, let's warm up the clam chowder," Lisa said as she made her way to the kitchen. Jennie and Peggy followed and soon they were all seated at the dining room table eating steaming bowls of clam chowder.

A fire was burning in the fireplace, and while Lisa put Sara to bed, Charlie got out the Scrabble board and decks of cards. The rain had stopped, and the wind had died down. "That's the end of the storm." Charlie said.

*****

The next morning they awoke to the cries of seagulls and the lapping of waves against the shore.

Peggy and Jeff decided to accompany Tom on his usual morning walk. The air was clear, and the sea was no longer dark and stormy although the waves still crashed with foam along the beach. The sun was already getting warm, and the smell of the sea was powerful. They walked along the beach dodging the crabs that emerged from the sand, and they sidestepped the seaweed, empty crab shells and bits of mussel shells that still littered the beach. The rest of the storm's debris had already been hauled away by the scavengers. There were a lot of smooth round pebbles that had been washed upon the sand, but now they were dry so they had lost their beauty. Sandpipers scurried along the beach close to the surf waiting for the sea to cast up their breakfast.

They watched as seagulls swooped down to pick up a clam then rise nearly thirty feet straight up in the air and drop the shell to break it open on the rocks. The ocean had returned to its normal blue-green color, and the sand was beginning to dry.

"Now I know why Charlie and Lisa like this place, there's never a dull moment, and the weather is close to perfect." Peggy said.

"Yes, it does have its charm. That's why your mother wants us to buy a summer home here. She's probably checking out the real estate section of the paper now," Tom replied.

"I've always heard that it only takes one trip to Cape Cod to be hooked forever. I'm beginning to believe it." Jeff said.

Peggy looked at her father and asked him if they really would buy a summer home here.

"We're seriously thinking about it, especially now that she's writing for the magazine. She thinks that you have to live here to write about it, and I rather like it myself. I can write and do what I do any place, I don't have to be in Chicago. It would be nice to get away from the city and come here for the summer. We've discussed it, and we can manage it."

"I think that's great, Dad, Jeff and I could visit you."

"That would be wonderful; we'd love to have you visit us any time. Now let's go back and have breakfast."

Everyone had finished their breakfast, and they were sitting around nursing mugs of coffee. Jennie rose and offered to scramble eggs for Tom, Peggy and Jeff, but they only wanted muffins and coffee. Charlie suggested they all do some sightseeing for the rest of the morning. "We can go to Provincetown and along the way tour an historic lighthouse. We could also stop in Brewster and visit the homes of famous sea captains. We'll take our van as it will seat all of us.

"Charlie, I'd like that, it sounds so interesting," Jennie said.

Jeff said, "Count me in; this is my first trip here so I'm anxious to see everything."

As they were piling into the van, Charlie told them he got it because they are constantly carrying things back and forth from the city. "We have even transported furniture. Whenever we come here the van is loaded."

They drove out of Barnstable and headed toward Provincetown along the ocean frontage road where the summer homes were. One house was more attractive than the other, and Jennie craned her neck to inspect each one. As she peered through the window, she saw the most beautiful house she had ever seen. 'I've seen this house before', she thought, and then she remembered. It was featured in the real estate section of Cape Cod Magazine under houses for sale. She asked Charlie to slow down, and he slowed to a crawl. There was a For Sale sign in the front yard, and a sign next to it said "Open House Today." "Oh, Charlie, pull over, I have to see this house." He drove onto the driveway, and they all got out and made their way up the front steps.

The real estate agent was pleased to see them, and she graciously offered to give them a tour of the house. It was a two-story house, sided with white clapboards with a generous wraparound porch. It had dusty blue shutters, and there were dormers in the upper story. The wide floorboards of the porch had weathered to an ageless gray. Jennie stood on the porch and looked across the lawn down to the shoreline and the beach. There were a few whitecaps on the ocean that appeared to be resting after last night's storm.

The realtor led them inside to the front room that was papered in a faded yellow paper that had come loose from the walls in spots. There were shades on the windows that reminded her of shades in old schoolrooms. It had been for sale for several years, and she wondered why. They climbed the stairs to the second story and entered one of the bedrooms that had bright lime green walls. The only item in the room was a red kitchen chair that had been painted with a fire-engine red lacquer. Lisa commented, "I like the chair." There were two other bedrooms each painted a different bright color. The single bathroom was all white.

Downstairs there was a good-sized pantry next to the kitchen, and Peggy commented, "This could be a powder room." The kitchen was smaller than she would have liked, and the refrigerator and stove would have to be replaced, but, Jennie beamed with happiness. Tom said, "If you like it, let's make an offer."

"Oh, honey, are you serious! It needs a lot of work, but I love it."

"I can see us living here, so let's go talk to the realtor and find out what it's listed at."

The realtor told them it was listed at $98,000, and Tom and Jennie offered $90,000. The realtor told them she would have to make a call. She called and was told the seller would not go lower than $92,000. Jennie looked at Tom as if to say, it's your decision. He thought for a moment and then said, "Let's take it." Jennie threw her arms around him and kissed him, then everyone threw their arms around them and they all stood hugging and laughing.

The realtor gave them a contract to sign, and Tom told her they were from Chicago. "That's okay, she said, all our sales are to out-of-towners. We do this all the time."

They continued on to Provincetown, past historic Federal houses that were old and weathered, the paint peeling, square mansions with widow's walks once the homes of ship captains, down Main Street with its narrow storefront shops aglow in Christmas lights, the first they had seen on the drive.

After touring a lighthouse, they stopped at a fish house called The Blue Schooner and ate fried cod sandwiches for lunch. The harbor was filled with lobster boats moored for the Christmas holiday, and the bar was crowded with fishermen and workers let off early from work. The fishermen's yellow slickers hung on hooks that lined the wall just inside the door, and the smell of the sea lingered in the air. One fisherman turned to the man next to him and said, "You pulled your boat early this year."

"Yes, the season is a bitch. I'm not making a dime this month."

The man nodded and said, "No one's making any money this time of year. You hear about the man in Truro?"

"No, what happened?"

"He was pulling in his pots and his foot got caught in the rope, and he went overboard. He died of a heart attack from the ice cold water before drowning."

"Oh, man," he mourned. "Kids?"

"Two small children."

"Oh, man."

The jukebox was loud and Bing Crosby was singing White Christmas, but no one was listening. The waitress brought steaming mugs of coffee, and the conversation returned to the house. Jennie had already made plans for its renovation. "We'll leave the upstairs bedrooms as they are for the time being. The first thing we'll do is get new appliances for the kitchen. The downstairs rooms will need to be painted."

"I'll do the painting," Tom said.

They attended Christmas Eve services at the old white wooden Congregational church not far from the harbor where it had stood for many generations. Its stately wooden spire could be seen for miles away. It was warm, brightly lit, and, the wide wood plank floor creaked as the worshippers made their way up the center aisle.

"Don't you almost feel like a pilgrim?" Lisa whispered to Jennie.

Jennie nodded as she looked around at the barrenness of the church. The organist began playing Joy to the World, and everyone rose and sang loudly and joyfully. The minister moved to the pulpit, and the church was hushed as the congregation took their seats. After the service they came back to the house for a light supper and to open presents. Charlie made a fire, and the hot coals from the fireplace filled the room with warmth. Sara amused herself, and soon the living room floor was strewn with colored paper and ribbons. After she had been put to bed, Tom poured champagne, and they sat around talking.

"I noticed there's a definite lack of Christmas commercialism in these Puritan towns that make up the Cape," Jeff commented.

"It's because we don't have shopping malls, and all the tourists have left. There are a lot of activities that begin after Thanksgiving. They're mainly family activities for the few residents who live here year-around. They have Christmas strolls, caroling, craft shows, chowder festivals, and, of course, the usual visit from Santa. The people here like to enjoy the charm and elegance of Christmas the way it used to be." Charlie said.

"There's a Flying Santa who visits all the remote lighthouses and drops off presents for the keepers and their family. It's a huge project, and it's been going on for about 80 years," Lisa added.

Jennie went to the window, and Tom joined her. They stood watching the moonlight on the water. "Now we'll have our own home on the water," he said.

"Tom, this is the most wonderful Christmas. Maybe we should always come to the Cape for Christmas."

They had planned to sleep late on Christmas morning, but Sara changed those plans. She woke at her usual early hour and began crying which woke everyone else. Lisa bathed her and dressed her in the yellow overall-style jeans with white long-sleeved T-shirt that Jennie and Tom gave her for Christmas. She also put on the white, high-topped shoes they gave her. Jennie had told them that she would soon be walking, and she should have a sturdy pair of shoes with firm soles.

Jennie picked her up and took her downstairs to the kitchen where Charlie was. "Hi, Pumpkin," Charlie said as he picked her up and set her on the counter. He kissed her cheek and inhaled the smell of baby powder. She was daddy's girl, and she liked his full attention.

Charlie made bacon and eggs for breakfast, and they all ate as if they were starving. "You better leave room for steaks for dinner," he told them. I'm going to broil steaks outside on the grill for Christmas dinner."

"There's a lot to like about living here, that wouldn't happen in Chicago," Tom commented.

Jeff had been eyeing his watch every ten minutes and finally Charlie flipped on the TV. The Chicago Bears were playing the New York Giants at Chicago. The games at Soldier's Field began at noon, and the three men were eager for the kick-off. The Bears were undefeated, and Jeff and Tom wanted it to stay that way. Charlie would cheer for the Giants although his allegiance was really with the Bears. Even though he lives in New York now, Chicago will always be home.

Jennie, Peggy and Lisa went to the kitchen. They prepared a tray of snacks and appetizers to tide them over until the game was over. For dinner they would have steak, baked potato, Caesar salad, and freshly-baked popovers, and for dessert they would have Christmas cookies and chocolate ice cream sundaes. At Charlie's insistence, Lisa had been experimenting with various recipes in order to create the perfect popover, and she felt she had succeeded. Charlie came into the kitchen to get drinks for everyone, and he announced, "Wait until you taste Lisa's popovers, they are the best!" She readied the pan and mixing bowl while Jennie cut up the salad greens, and Peggy set the table. There was a roar and a groan from the living room, and they knew the Bears had scored. "That's as much as we can do now, let's go join the guys." Lisa said.

They watched the Bears score the first touchdown, and they watched as the Giants pounced on them, and the half ended with the Bears down 24-7.

"Don't even think about dinner, we've got to see this game to the end," Tom said. They opened another can of beer and reached for the chips and dip.

When the second half started all the fans in Soldier's Field were charged, there was electricity in the air. Then the Bears held the Giants and blocked their punt. The comeback had begun, and Tom and Jeff were cheering loudly. Even Charlie knew there was no turning back, and he cheered for the Bears, too.

They watched from their living room on Cape Cod as the Chicago Bears came back, overtook the Giants, and remained undefeated.

After dinner as they sat around eating their dessert, they were quietly thinking that another Christmas celebration was winding down. It had been a glorious weekend and tomorrow they would be heading home.

"Should we all meet here again next year?" Charlie asked.

"Yes, let's, they said in unison."

Chapter Twenty

Peggy couldn't wait to get to the shop to find out what business had come in while she was at the Cape and to select paint chips and fabric samples for their penthouse apartment. She and Jeff had discussed color preferences for each room, and she lost no time in selecting the appropriate samples. She was going to spend the weekend with him at his Lake Forest home, and she wanted to have everything ready to take with her. They would need new furniture, and she selected brochures from some of the furniture showrooms in the Merchandise Mart. When she felt she had everything they would need, she piled it all in the back seat of her old Chevrolet Impala and left. Traffic was heavy on the expressway, and the excitement of spending two days and nights with Jeff made it difficult to concentrate, but she stayed calm and was mentally alert to the traffic situation.

When she drove up his street and turned onto his driveway she was surprised to see a pale yellow Mercedes parked near the house. Jeff hurried out the front door, and Peggy asked him if he had visitors.

"No, I don't, this is yours," He said as he put his arm around her. "It was supposed to be your Christmas present, but I wasn't able to get delivery in time. Do you like it?"

"Jeff, are you serious, I can't believe it!"

"Yes, I'm serious, it's yours." He put both arms around her and drew her close. He felt tears on her cheek. "Why are you crying?"

Sobbing, she said, "I'm over-whelmed, I'm happy."

He kissed her and held her close until she recovered and was smiling. "I love you, she whispered."

They brought the samples in from the car and left them in the foyer. They could wait until tomorrow.

Jeff asked her whether she wanted to eat in or go out for dinner. "Let's cook something here," Peggy said.

The refrigerator was practically empty since his mother was going to be gone for sometime. "It looks as though we will either have to eat out or grocery shop."

"Let's go shopping. We'll need something for breakfast and the rest of the weekend."

"I was very busy at the office all week and didn't have time to do much else. I'm sorry."

"That's okay; we'll get what we want. Besides, I planned to have you all to myself this weekend."

"I like your plans. Do they include making love?"

"Definitely," she said.

They laughed as they went up and down the aisles picking up impulse items they usually resisted like potato chips and dip and Ben & Jerry's ice cream, they shopped the produce and meat departments, filling the cart with more than they would possibly use. While they were picking up eggs and milk, two women were off to the side watching them. They overheard one woman say to the other,

"That's Jeffrey Burnham; they say he killed his wife." Both Jeff and Peggy froze, momentarily not knowing whether to look at them or not. Jeff was visibly hurt, and Peggy put her arm in his and kissed him on the cheek. "Let's leave, don't even look at them," she said.

Jeff quietly said, "I guess this wasn't such a good idea, I'm sorry you had to hear it."

"I can't believe people can be so hateful and mean," she said.

"I wonder how long it will take…Having you at my side makes it all bearable."

*****

After a dinner of pasta with broccoli, salad, a crusty bread, and a red wine, they played Scrabble in front of the fireplace. They put the board on a coffee table, and they sat cross-legged on the floor. They were both skilled players, but Jeff became distracted from looking at Peggy's knit top that clung snugly to her breasts revealing plenty of skin. When Jeff got up to pour more wine, he came behind her, put his arms around her and told her how gorgeous she was. Peggy just smiled and kept looking at her letters.

Later Jeff told her it was too distracting playing with a beautiful woman, and he led her up the stairs to his bedroom.

In the morning they awoke together, smiled and made love again, then showered and went downstairs to make breakfast. During the weekend they spent hours talking and learning so much more about each other. They discovered they had so much more in common than they had thought, and it was a toss-up as to who did the most talking. On Monday he sent flowers to her at work, and he had the florist write on the card, "Flowers for the most tenderhearted and amazing woman I've ever met."

That night he took her out for dinner, and after they finished she blew him a kiss across the table. They put on their coats, paid the bill, and headed outside only to find it had been snowing. They slowly walked to the car in the lightly falling snow. He told her how beautiful she was with the snow falling on her long brown hair, and as always they were reluctant to part.

*****

Both Peggy and Jeff were very busy with their jobs, but they found time to meet at the apartment to inspect and supervise the work that was being done. The painters and other tradesmen were well known to Peggy through Levine Interiors, and she could give them instructions on what needed to be done and then leave them unsupervised. In between their jobs and the renovation, they sandwiched time to shop for furniture. They decided they would buy all their furniture locally. It saved time, and they wanted to support local businesses. They also had to make decisions on bathroom fixtures and kitchen appliances.

The old wall to wall carpeting in several rooms was torn up and replaced by dark wood flooring. Area rugs were required, and if they didn't find what they liked locally, they went to the Merchandise Mart where they could order directly from the mills. They didn't settle for anything they didn't like in order to have something in place; they decided to go without until they found what they wanted.

They met with Rev. Robinson at the First Presbyterian Church in Lincoln Park where Peggy was baptized, and the wedding was scheduled for Saturday, May 15th. The reception would be held at the Drake Hotel in Chicago. Her parents were married at the same church, and they had their reception at the Drake. Jennie recalled the hotel's beautiful décor and their delicious food and suggested that Peggy and Jeff also have their reception there. It was a Chicago landmark and elegant in every way. They would have cocktails in the Venetian Room which overlooked the lake, and they reserved the small ballroom for dinner and dancing.

Beth returned from Florida to help Peggy with arrangements. She knew a Chinese woman in Chinatown who did beautiful calligraphy and was reasonable. They decided to have her address the wedding invitations.

Peggy suggested that she and Jennie and Beth shop together for their dresses. They would make a day of it and have lunch at the Walnut Room at Fields. Jennie and Beth decided they did not want the timeworn pastel mother-of-the bride/groom dresses. They wanted brighter, more flattering colors, and Peggy wholeheartedly agreed with them. Beth selected a bright blue shade which was very attractive with her silver hair, and Jennie found a green dress that was stunning on her. Lisa was going to wear a rose-colored dress with spaghetti straps. Peggy went to three stores before she found the dress she had in mind at Neiman-Marcus. It was strapless with a fitted embroidered bodice and slightly flared ankle-length skirt. Her veil was shoulder length. She wanted a dress that would be comfortable for dancing because they had arranged to have Stanley Paul and his Orchestra play at their reception. He played wonderful dance music, and his orchestra was very popular and always in demand in Chicago. Peggy and Jeff liked to dance, and Stanley Paul's orchestra would be a highlight of the evening.

Finally the long-awaited day arrived, and Peggy and Jeff were married at the Presbyterian Church in Lincoln Park that she had attended all her life. It was a rainy day, and Jennie told her that was a sign they would have many children. Peggy quipped, "We probably will if we aren't careful." It was a small wedding, about 60 guests, and it took place at 4 o'clock in the chapel. From there they went directly to the Drake for the reception.

Charlie, Lisa, and Sara had flown in from New York, and they were staying with Jennie and Tom. They hired a baby sitter to stay with Sara for the evening. Jennie and Tom's table at the reception included Matt and Suz Shapiro, Lauren and Peter who were now Dr. and Mrs. Adler, and Beth Burnham. Charlie and Lisa shared the bride and groom's table. In keeping with tradition, Tom led the bride to the dance floor for the first dance and Jeff cut in to applause from the guests. The father/daughter song that was played was "Daddy's

Little Girl," and Stanley Paul played "Because You Loved Me" when Jeff cut in. Of course, the orchestra's lovely, talented vocalist sang both songs.

After the reception which lasted well into the evening, the bride and groom went to their new apartment and left for Florence, Italy the following day. After their two-week honeymoon, they returned to their jobs and their penthouse apartment. They vowed not to make any immediate changes in their lives.

Peggy told her parents, "Florence is the most romantic foreign city I've ever seen."

"It's the only foreign city you've seen," Jennie reminded her.

"Every evening after dinner, Jeff and I strolled along the River Arno. It was beautiful. I felt like a different person in Italy. Tuscany was very beautiful. There was so much to see. The art galleries and quaint little shops were wonderful. And we met some fascinating people. One young couple was going to Cairo to dig for buried artifacts and treasures. I've had more excitement in the month I've been married than in the rest of my life."

"Honey, I hope it will always be that way," Jennie said.

*****

The following day Jennie and Tom left to go to their new home on the Cape. They had gone earlier in March before wedding activities would prevent them from leaving. They had painted the dining room and living room a sunny yellow, and because it was so small, they painted the kitchen white including the cabinets. They had shopped for a refrigerator and stove and had them installed. Now they saw the need for a microwave oven so that was on their to-do list. At Peggy's suggestion, they had turned the large pantry into a powder room. The walls and floor tiles were blue to compliment the sea, and the fixtures and towels were white. Now they won't have to run up the stairs whenever they need to go to the bathroom. Their advancing ages dictated that reasoning. Suz and Matt were coming to spend a week with them, and they wanted to have everything they would need for their comfort and enjoyment. The cupboards and refrigerator needed to be stocked with dishes and food. They packed the car with things such as dishes and pots and pans that they no longer needed here and that would now be utilized at the Cape.

They woke early and ate breakfast so they could get in a good driving day before they stopped in early evening. Tom had studied his maps and said it would be a full two-day drive to Boston. West Seneca, New York was the halfway point, and that is where they would stay overnight. From Boston they would take Route 3 to the Sagamore Bridge to cross the canal and then Route 6 to Barnstable They were excited and anxious to be "Cape Codders," but they also felt some melancholy and apprehension about leaving Chicago for three or four months. They had never been away from home that long before.

The trip was pleasant and uneventful until they reached the Sagamore Bridge where they could see low clouds and fog. They turned the radio on, and the announcer said that the dense fog and clouds covering the Cape were expected to come and go throughout the weekend with a smattering of sun on Sunday. By Monday it would be clear and sunny. It was Saturday so Tom expected to be driving through some really dense fog. At times the fog was so dense and he was so tense that he almost dug his fingernails into the steering wheel. They could hear the mournful sound of fog horns on ships in the harbor alerting others to their presence.

"Thank God, traffic is light," Tom muttered.

"Sensible people stay off the roads," Jennie quipped.

It was a little eerie not being able to see and at the same time hear the fog horn warnings. But the fog was patchy and at times it almost lifted completely, lending a note of charm to the sleepy fishing villages.

It was late in the day when they arrived, and when they entered their new home they were almost overwhelmed from the smell of paint. The house had been closed since they were there painting in March. They opened all the windows and unpacked the car. Tom went into town to get some pizza while Jennie unpacked the sheets and blankets and made their bed. After eating they decided to go for a short walk to stretch their legs and get some air. Everything else could wait until tomorrow.

Walking through the murky atmosphere on the beach, the only sound was the low drone of fog horns.

"Do people get used to that?" Jennie asked.

"Tomorrow you won't even hear it. It's a part of everyday life when you live on the ocean, and the ocean is the lifeblood of Cape Cod. I imagine that sound can be very reassuring to the fishermen who make their living from the ocean." Tom replied.

The following week Suz and Matt arrived. They loved Jennie and Tom's new home and were anxious to see and do everything Cape Cod had to offer. The July issue of Cape Cod magazine was lying on the coffee table, and Suz picked it up and began leafing through it. It was the "Best of Cape Cod" issue, and she was hooked. They all decided to try as many of the "best picks" as possible.

"Let's check out the clam chowder," Matt suggested.

"I want to taste the Lobster Ice Cream," Suz said.

"I'd like to take the whale-watching boat trip," Tom chimed in.

"Brewster is known for its old sea captain's homes and some are open to the public. I'd like to take that tour," Jennie said.

"Barnstable has pizza parlors like every Main Street, but it has cafes that serve steaming platters of mussels and Italian ices with flat wooden spoons glued to their lids," she added.

For two days the friends drove up and down Route 6 visiting the various towns and villages that made up the Cape. On the third day they took their coffee and muffins to the front porch and sat looking out at the ocean and the beach. The ocean was calm and bright blue with not a cloud or a seagull in sight.

"Let's go to the beach today," Suz said. "It's going to be a perfect day for sunbathing."

"Yes, it would be nice to have a relaxing day. We've been on the go every minute that you've been here," Jennie replied.

They took their large red and white striped beach umbrellas, towels, and a large thermos of lemonade and staked their claim on the sandy beach. Soon it would be crowded with tourists and vacationers with white arms and legs who want to be tan and lovely to fit in with the crowds of glamorous tourists roaming the streets and filling the cafes. After they had coated each other with suntan oil,

Tom and Matt decided to walk the beach close to the water so they could feel the waves softly lapping the sand. Jennie and Suz wanted to lie on the sand with their eyes closed and bake until they needed to cool off. At first the water was icy cold and they shrieked with laughter. Then they braved the cold and plunged in head first. They were numb when they emerged, and the hot sun felt good as they again spread out in the sand.

"We may have a grandchild soon," Suz said. "Lauren and Peter want a child but she is having difficulty conceiving. They have been seeing a fertility specialist so we hope to hear good news soon. It does happen to many couples, but we never expected it would be a problem for them. They desperately want to have a child who is a part of them so adoption isn't an option now. Peter is very devoted to Lauren; we know they want their own."

"Peter has always been devoted to Lauren. I remember when they were teenagers and dating. He was so proud and happy to be with her," Jennie said.

"At first we wondered what she saw in him. He was tall and skinny with perpetual acne, and when he walked it was as if his feet got in the way, but Lauren adored him. He was smart and he was very mature for his age. I think Lauren felt protected and loved when she was with him. Now look at him, a tall, handsome, successful heart doctor. Sometimes our kids know more than we give them credit for."

"That's very true," Jennie replied. "I remember when Charlie brought Lisa home to meet us; she was a real surprise with her tattoo and dreadlocks. Immediately I wondered what he saw in her and if he was truly serious about her. But she is the most wonderful wife and mother, and Charlie couldn't be happier. Neither could we."

"Peggy also was a concern. We worried about her involvement with Jeff Burnham when his first wife died from drugs and his alleged suspicion of murder. But she stood by him, she knew he would be acquitted and eventually freed from guilt. Those two are so much in love; I hope they will always love each other as much as they do now."

"Yes, it's evident they are in love. Its fun to be in their presence and see and feel the love they have for each other," Suz said.

"It's amusing for Tom and me, too. They're going to China next week. Jeff has to go on business, but they're going to do some sightseeing.

When they return they are coming here for a long weekend, and with Charlie and Lisa here for the summer, our family will all be together again."

Tom and Matt returned, each carrying a yellow and red paper bag. Tom said, "We walked a couple of miles down the beach and spotted a Dairy Queen so we stopped and bought lunch. Thought you gals would be getting hungry. When we started out, the beach was practically empty, but coming back it's already crowded. We walked past some beautiful year-round homes and some small vacation cottages along the beach. Tomorrow let's rent some bicycles and ride around Barnstable or we could drive to Truro and see the huge sand dunes. They're something to see! Actually, if you're up to it, we could do both."

"That's a good possibility," Jennie said. "But tonight let's go to Moby Dicks for a lobster dinner. We might have to wait in line, but it's worth it."

The next day they decided to drive in the opposite direction on Route 6 and visit Sandwich and Plymouth, two of the oldest towns on the Cape. It was hot and humid so they dressed in sandals, shorts and tees. They toured the glass museum and bought some pieces of glass at the Sandwich Glass Factory showroom. The Annual Red, White &

Blueberry festival was in full swing, and local farmers proudly displayed their blue gems. The festival also included an art show. Jennie and Suz spied an artist who sold hand-crafted jewelry, and they did not walk away empty handed. The clam chowder cook-off seemed like a good idea since it was lunch time. They sampled and tasted every entry, and Tom was the only one who picked the winning entry.

Next, they bought double-dip ice cream cones and walked to the harbor to watch the boats entering and leaving. The oppressive heat drove everyone to the water so there was a lot of activity. They noticed the sign, "Whale-Watching Tours," and Tom said, "Hey, guys, I'd really like to take one of those tours, wouldn't you?"

"Yes, let's go and cool off." Matt replied.

A big beautiful ship was boarding several passengers, and they got in line. After everyone had boarded, they glided out of the harbor with an escort of gulls overhead flapping their wings. A guide welcomed them on board and told them they would be within feet of the most graceful, rare mammals in the world. He further stated they would cruise to the whale's favorite feeding grounds so they would be assured of seeing several whales, and if lucky, they would see a whale breach.

"What's that," Suz whispered to Matt.

"Breaching is when a whale shoots straight up out of the water and splashes down again into the sea."

The ship glided smoothly over the ocean for about a half hour and then the guide told them they were in the feeding area. "Keep an eye out because one could pop up at any moment," he said. A hushed silence fell as all eyes watched the water off the sides of the boat. Then with a loud roar, up came a whale as she let a large gush of water out her blowhole. The children cheered and then were quiet as the giant whale then flipped back into the water lifting her tail for all to see. The children and adults alike peered over the railing trying to get a peek at the huge whale lurking below the water's surface.

The guide told them the most common whale in their area is the humpback that averages about 50 feet in length, however, they have seen them as long as 120 feet. Then they saw several whales diving in and out of the water as if they were playing a game. The children shrieked and cheered as they watched them frolic in the water. All at once there was a loud roar from the water as a gigantic whale leaped high in the air and then sunk down gracefully into the water.

Everyone became very quiet, they were too astonished to speak, and then another whale on the other side of the ship leaped high into the air and splashed down into the sea. It was as if they had been trained to perform their act.

The guide said, “Well, folks, today we got lucky. Its not often we see two whales breach on a tour. As I said, we’re usually lucky to see one.”

As they were cruising back to the dock, Jennie said, “I’m really glad we did this, I had no idea we would see a whale leap out of the water.”

“I thought the tour would be worth seeing,” Tom replied.

“We’d like to take you out for dinner tonight. Where will it be?” Matt said.

“We talked about going to Alberto’s, but we didn’t make it. Would that be okay?” Jennie asked.

“I’d love to go to Alberto’s. We’ve been eating so much fish, Italian sounds great.” Matt said.

While they were eating, Tom said, "There's more to the Cape than pristine ocean beaches. There's a nature preserve off of Route 6 where nature is not under man's control. Let's hike through it tomorrow. You won't see a perfectly mowed lawn, but you will see hiking trails surrounded by prairie grass, wildflowers, untamed brush and wildlife. It's a part of the Cape that most tourists ignore because they just come for the beaches."

"Let's do that, let's get away from the commercialism and see other features of Cape Cod," Matt replied.

As they walked along, out of some underbrush ahead of the path, a baby deer sprung out, looked them over, and then quietly glided off into the marsh. What a beautiful animal! As they walked on to where the baby deer had come from, they came across the carcass of a deer that evidently was the baby's mother.

"Oh, how sad," they moaned. The baby deer was on its own now. They wished it a life free of danger.

They oohed and aahed as they continued to explore and enjoy the beauty of the preserve. Then they entered an open area where they could see the ocean off to their left. The sky was blue, and the ocean was as blue as the sky. Suddenly a bad-tempered blue jay was screeching overhead, and they saw that he was chasing a rabbit. He scolded and repeatedly dived at the rabbit that was desperately running for cover. They stopped and Jennie and Suz cheered him on. "Hurry, hurry, find some cover! Run faster!" Then the rabbit made its way into some thick underbrush and was safe. They clapped their hands secure in the thought that they had saved its life.

The blue jay flew to a nearby tree to roost and catch its breath. As they got closer he began screeching and scolding them. They stopped and stood looking up and talking to him. Jennie let out a screech as she felt stings on her ankle. She looked down to see that she was standing on an ant hill. That was the end of their nature walk.

While walking back to the car, Suz and Matt told Jennie and Tom they were sad to be leaving tomorrow; they wished they could stay there forever.

"You can always come back; we'd love to see you any time. In fact, I insist you come back next summer. Let's make it a ritual." Jennie said.

"I promise we will come back," Suz replied.

Tom and Jennie told them they were going to stay at the Cape through Christmas. "We decided to celebrate both Thanksgiving and Christmas here, and both Tom and I need some quiet time for writing, so we might as well do our writing here rather than go home to Chicago and then have that long drive back for Thanksgiving." "Sounds like the smart thing to do, but I'll miss you. We won't see each other until January. By that time we should have lots of news to share," Suz replied.

*****

After their friends left, Jennie sat down to do some serious writing. She had a deadline to meet at Cape Cod Magazine, and she decided to write a story about their week with Suz and Matt. It would be a recommendation of how to explore and enjoy Cape Cod in a week. She told about their sight-seeing trips, including the whale-watching cruise, the restaurants and the food they ate, the merchandise the various shops had to offer, the museums where they learned the history of the Cape, and where to find the most beautiful beaches. She was confident that their readers would enjoy the story.

Peggy called and told them they were flying to Boston and renting a car for the drive to the Cape and they would arrive late Thursday afternoon in time for dinner. They would be with them on Friday and Saturday and leave on Sunday for their return to Chicago. It was their first summer visit to the Cape and they wanted to enjoy the outdoor life as much as much as possible. Tom made a list of things to see and do including a whale-watching cruise. They were anxious to hear all about Jeff and Peggy's trip to China. Charlie and Lisa and Sara would join them for dinner Thursday evening, and Jennie and Tom looked forward to having their family together for the weekend.

After they were settled in and were enjoying wine and appetizers on the front porch, Tom asked Peggy, "So what did you think of China?" She said, "It was crowded and noisy, it was gaudy. It was quiet and serene, it was beautiful. I've never seen such contrasts in one place."

She went on to say that the people were friendly and very polite, and she was surprised to learn that the women control the purse strings.

Charlie made a humorous comment that the Chinese women have become "westernized."

Jeff told about his tour of a manufacturing plant in Beijing and how open the Chinese people are now concerning new techniques and methods of producing their products.

"I've been interested in China for a long time. In fact, several years ago I wrote a book on the economic growth of China. If you'd like to read it, I have some copies at home in Chicago. I'll give you a copy." Tom said.

"Yes, I'd like to read it. I didn't know you wrote a book on China."

"Dinner is ready, please come to the dining room," Jennie announced. On the table was a platter of succulent yellow ears of corn surrounded by lobster salad and warm freshly baked rolls. "We're having strawberry shortcake for dessert."

While they were eating they discussed the weekend's activities. Tom told them about the whale-watching cruise and the Cape Cod National

Seashore Park at Provincetown. The massive sand dunes and white beaches are awesome, and everyone agreed that they would be worth seeing. Tom suggested they do that on Friday before the weekenders arrive and lines form at every landmark and restaurant.

"I highly recommend a whale-watching tour; I guarantee you'll not be disappointed, and he told them about seeing two whales breach on their tour last week. I admit that I'm becoming a nerdy whale-loving fan," Tom said.

"You make it sound great; I don't want to pass it up." Peggy said.

"I agree, let's go look for whales," Jeff replied.

"I'm glad you agree. We'll drive to Provincetown near the whale feeding area. It's the best spot, and we can sightsee along the way."

After they boarded the boat, the guide told them they could get up and move around once they were out of the harbor. They had gone a short distance when they were amazed to see 25 or 30 humpback whales and two Minke whales all swimming together. The captain carefully maneuvered the boat for the best viewing from all sides so that all the passengers got to see the whales putting on their show. They came right up to the boat where Peggy and Jeff were standing, and they seemed to be putting on a show just for them. The passengers Ooohed and Aaahhed as the whales came up right to the boat. One whale slapped the water repeatedly with its tail next to the boat, and the guide said "that's 30 tons of power." Another kept spinning and turning while another whale turned on its side and slapped the water with its fin. Another whale breached right in front of them, and they were sprayed with water.

"That's awesome, I can't believe how fun-loving they are," Peggy said.

"They were close enough to touch. What a site!" Jeff exclaimed

"We were lucky; you got to see a real show, a much better sighting than we saw last week. The guide said he'd never seen so many at one time before," Jennie said.

"Pretty damned amazing; they are so majestic and graceful," Tom said.

On the way back, they drove through the National Seashore Park and saw sand dunes 100 feet high and the whitest, most pristine beaches. They all agreed that it would be fun to hike or bicycle through the enormous park some day.

"There's lots to see right here in Barnstable, and they have an open-air tour bus that takes you for a ride all over town. It's an hour tour, and a guide points out highlights and things of interest. We could do that if you'd like," Jennie said.

"Could we do that tomorrow morning and then spend the afternoon at the beach?" Peggy asked.

It was a hot, sunny August afternoon, perfect beach weather. They decided to walk along the shore to look for sea shells and sea glass. They were deep in conversation, and Sara amused herself by watching the fiddler crabs flit in and out of holes in the sand. She was afraid to touch them, but she was fascinated by their shape and the way they suddenly appeared out of the sand. She would run ahead of the others although they watched her and called her back if she went too far ahead. Suddenly her red T-shirt flashed in the surf as it was receding from the shore. The undertow was taking her out to sea. Charlie and Jeff who happened to see her at the same time, raced toward her and Charlie snatched her like a small dog from the surf. He held her face down by the waist as if he was shaking her dry, and she began sputtering and crying. She coughed and shivered from the cold sea water, and Charlie and Jeff immediately stripped her of her wet clothes and wrapped her in their shirts which were warm from their body heat. "Let's hurry back, in a minute she'll be freezing," Charlie shouted. He cradled her in his arms to warm her, and they all rushed home. Lisa had concealed her anguish, but now she cried openly over the thought of what might have happened if Charlie and Jeff hadn't seen her in time. She wrapped Sara in warm blankets and rubbed her arms and legs to stop the shivering. When she felt warm all over and was no longer shivering, Lisa hugged and kissed her and rocked her to sleep.

Everyone had feelings of guilt as they mentally replayed the tragedy that could have in a split second taken little Sara from them.

Tom said, "We should have been watching her more closely."

"We shouldn't have let her play so close to the water's edge," Jennie said.

Sara slept for awhile, and when she woke she was her usual happy and playful self. Gradually everyone lightened and things returned to normal.

*****

After dinner, they took their coffee to the living room to relax and watch a beautiful sunset. Jeff surprised everyone when he told them they were thinking of buying a home on the Cape. "Peggy and I have fallen in love with this place, and we'd like to call it our second home. We understand now why you keep coming back here. Once you've experienced all it has to offer, it's difficult to walk away from this life."

Charlie said, "We wondered if you would be hooked like we were when we first came here."

"It wouldn't be a bad investment; year around homes are becoming hard to find. There isn't much land left so there's very little new building. We'll do some looking, and Jen has gotten to know a realtor fairly well, so we'll ask her to be on the lookout," Tom replied.

"That would be great; we'll be back for Thanksgiving so we could look at some homes then. Of course, we'd like to be on the water just as you are," Jeff replied.

"We wouldn't need any more space than you have, and I like being close to the beach," Peggy said. "We'd like to be in this same area in Barnstable."

"We'll start looking right away. It would be nice if we could all be near each other," Jennie said.

After a delicious breakfast, Peggy and Jeff took one last walk down to the beach to enjoy one last gaze at the ocean with beautiful white caps racing to the shore. They didn't want to leave, but they knew they would be back. Then they said good-bye to Jennie and Tom and left for the trip home to Chicago.

Chapter Twenty-One

A small yellow Mercedes was often seen winding its way up and down the North Shore as Peggy went on her sales calls. Beth had recommended her to all her friends, and the name Peggy Doyle quickly became a household word in Winnetka, Wilmette, Lake Forest and many towns and villages beyond. She was making more money than she had expected. They had finished rehabbing and furnishing their penthouse apartment, and their love for each other grew more each day. They cooked elaborate dinners and ate them by candlelight. They made love for hours. After making love, he held her in his arms. He told her he would never leave her. He always slept with his arm draped over her.

One day when Jeff returned home from work, he told Peggy that he had to go to Beijing again. "The part that we are getting from them is not being machined to the proper tolerance, and it's a matter that cannot be handled by phone. Can you get away to go with me?" he asked knowing her extremely busy schedules.

"Of course, I'll go, I love China, I can always rearrange my appointments. When will we leave?"

"We'll leave Saturday afternoon. I have an early Monday morning appointment. We can have some time to ourselves on Sunday."

"That sounds perfect. I'll do some shopping while you are in meetings. I'd like to look at some silk fabrics, and I'd like to employ a shopping tour guide to show me around and be my interpreter. A person can waste a lot of time when they don't know where to go to get the best quality for the price."

"You're becoming quite the business woman; you constantly amaze me, and I'm happy you're still an attractive, sexy woman. Don't ever change."

They flew directly to Beijing from O'Hare. It was a twelve-hour flight, and they took an overnight flight arriving in Beijing in time for a lunch of soup and dumplings. "That's what everyone eats for lunch, Jeff told her. "As soon as you're seated, a waiter rushes to your table with a basket of steaming dumpling soup." It was Sunday, and the streets were crowded with sightseers. They took a cruise on the Yangtze River and walked to Tiananmen Square, which was jammed with people and security guards. Since they were still feeling the effects of jet lag they had a light dinner and went to bed early.

On Monday morning, Jeff took a taxi to the manufacturing plant, and Peggy went to see the concierge to line up a tour guide. The guide took Peggy to a huge market that had fabrics, jewelry, jeans, silk scarves, leather purses, T shirts, CD's and DVD's, watches, art, - you name it, they had it. Sue, her guide, told Peggy, "Bargaining is an art here and everyone bargains, so I will do the bargaining for you." Peggy was extremely happy with that arrangement as the only English they understood was "cheaper, good quality, how much you pay, and no profit." "Sue was worth every penny," she told Jeff.

On Tuesday morning, they went to see the Great Wall and in the afternoon they departed for home. They were just beginning to get the hang of China when they had to leave, but they were anxious to get back among speakers of the English language, sandwiches, and toilet paper.

As Peggy and Jeff were going through the accumulation of mail that had arrived in their absence, Peggy took the October issue of **Cape Cod Magazine** and went to her favorite chair to read her mother's article. Sometimes it was the only thing she read in the magazine. The story began…

"You must come to Cape Cod in October. Fall is a marvelous time of year on the Cape; the summer crowds have gone back to the cities, and the Codders reclaim their streets and their beaches, and their way of life that brought them here in the first place. Traffic no longer crawls through town, and we no longer have to wait for tables in the restaurants.

Nothing is complicated or fancy here, just practical and friendly. Tom and I recognize that every thing we want is here on the Cape. This is where we belong. The kids may travel far and wide, but for us, this is contentment.

Yesterday was a typical sunny, brisk day, and Tom walked to the barber shop for a trim and some "story telling or words of wisdom." The barber who was born here is now in his eighties. The calm of the place is comforting, and when he entered he said, "Ben, just thought I'd come and pass the time of day." Whatever was said about other people never left the shop.

Next, he went to the post office where other Codders were assembled and sharing the news of the day.

An expedition to the barber shop and post office takes up a large part of the day. That's the way it is off-season on the Cape, but when summer arrives, we all welcome the transfusion in the economy when the tourists once again take over this special piece of America. The sun drives them to the beaches, and the rain drives them to the shops to buy souvenirs.

Some out-of-towners come back for the fall foliage. The sumac is the first to turn red followed by the purple reds of the huckleberry. The scarlet red oak leaves have turned a brilliant red. The white oaks are the first to die, and they are beginning to curl up like stiff, ancient hands. The maples are brilliant in reds and yellows. Soon leaves are everywhere: on the sidewalks, on top of cars, caught in roof gutters and sewage drains. It's a wonderful time of year for long walks, and we want to be a part of it.

In April, when the buds on the oak trees are a little fatter and the pine needles a little greener, the residents also feel a sense of renewal. They get out their paint cans and brushes, and the cleanup begins. The outdoor tables and chairs are scrubbed clean of winter's grime, and workers are everywhere fixing and painting, getting ready for the spring and summer ahead.

In late afternoon a swirling orange forms in the west and a gorgeous sunset is forming underneath lowering clouds. It's the end of another wonderful day on Cape Cod."

"I love the way mother writes," she said to Jeff as she handed the magazine to him.

"Yes, she loves Cape Cod, and it's evident in her writing.

"I hope we can find a home near them, so we can just walk or bicycle back and forth.

"That would be ideal, but more importantly, we want to be on the ocean. Being inland would not be near as much fun."

"Yes, it's nice to just walk down to the beach and not have to drive someplace and walk a distance to get to the beach. Dad says that fall is perfect beach weather – no crowds, no humidity, no blazing sun, and flying insects. All you need take to the beach is a blanket, sunglasses, water, and some reading material. He says you can meander barefoot for hours along the beach and not see a soul, and the sunsets are absolutely beautiful."

"It sounds great, but remember; he is retired. Do you think they'll ever decide to leave Chicago and live there year around?"

"I don't know, sometimes I think they are moving in that direction, but then I think of our home in Lincoln Park and how much they've always loved that place since they completely renovated it. I think it would be difficult for them to walk away from it."

"You just reminded me of something; I hope we won't have to spend thousands of dollars on our home there before we put a stick of furniture in it."

Peggy laughed and said, "No, that won't happen; we want our beach house to be a casual place that doesn't require a lot of cleaning."

"Yeah, nothing more than the sand that can't be avoided."

"Exactly, after all, we'll be on vacation when we're there."

*****

A month after they returned from China, Peggy was feeling out of sorts, and she hadn't had her period. She was worried that she might be pregnant, but she didn't want to say anything to Jeff until she knew for sure. He was anxious to have children, and she didn't want to disappoint him. She waited a couple of weeks and then made an appointment with a gynecologist whose name was Dr. David Hammond. He tested her and told her she was indeed pregnant. After a thorough examination, he told her that her pelvic structure was too small for a vaginal delivery. "Your pelvis is very small, Mrs. Burnham, you weren't built to have babies."

"I just want a healthy baby," Peggy replied.

"You are a healthy woman; I see no reason why you shouldn't have a healthy baby. We'll set you up for periodic examinations. The nurse will make the appointments for you."

When she left his office, she didn't know whether to laugh or cry. She wasn't expecting to be pregnant so soon, they had only been married a few months. How should she tell Jeff? Should they go out for an intimate dinner? No, she thought, I'll just tell him when he comes home from work.

When Jeff walked through the door, he greeted her with his usual greeting, "Hi, beautiful, did you have a nice day?"

"I went to see a doctor," and for some strange reason, she couldn't continue.

He took her in his arms and said, "Are you trying to tell me something? Are we going to have a baby?"

"Yes, it happened in China, I'm almost two months pregnant."

"That's wonderful, honey." Then he began to laugh, "Made in China – my son was made in China. That's rich!"

"We don't know whether it's a boy or a girl. In two months we can have the fetus tested. Do you want to know in advance?"

"No, let's let nature take its course. I like surprises."

He kissed and hugged her again and asked, "Have you told your parents?"

"No, let's wait and surprise everybody at Thanksgiving, its only 2 weeks away."

Then the phone rang and Peggy took the call. "Hi, Mom, how are you and Dad?"

"We're fine, I was just calling to tell you that your father was out walking today and he came across a house that was just put on the market. It's about 5 blocks from here. It's an old Cape Cod that has had an addition put on it. He said it looks good from the outside. There was no one there, so we'll have to call the realtor to look at it. We could do that tomorrow, if it's okay with you and Jeff."

"Mom, that's wonderful. We could look at it Thanksgiving weekend. If you think we should put an offer on it so it doesn't sell between now and then, we will. Jeff is shaking his head yes, so let us know as soon as you can."

"This is so exciting. Dad was out walking today and came across a house that was just put on the market. It's about 5 blocks from them, and he said it looks good from the outside."

"That's encouraging, if a house is well cared for on the outside, usually it's in good shape inside. I'm anxious to hear what they have to tell us."

The following day Jennie called back and talked to Peggy. "Peggy, you are going to love it. It's a typical Cape Cod house where you'd expect to see geraniums in the window and jellies on the shelves. It's a white clapboard with pale green shutters, a small front porch, and inside, a great room with stone fireplace, kitchen, pantry and bedroom on the first floor and three bedrooms and bath upstairs."

"What is the kitchen like?" Peggy asked.

"The kitchen has been updated with gas stove, refrigerator, dish washer, and microwave. The cabinets are oak with white countertops. The kitchen isn't large, but it's well laid out, very workable. It has a beige linoleum floor. The best thing about the kitchen is that the appliances are new, and that is something you have to equate to dollars and cents."

"How big is the pantry – could it be made into a powder room?"

"Yes, there's room for a toilet and sink. The great room is wallpapered and it has dark woodwork."

"We can change that. What about upstairs?"

"The bedrooms have wall paper and the woodwork is dark. The only bad thing is that there are old iron bedsteads in two bedrooms. Evidently the previous owners took the easy way out and just left them for someone else to deal with."

"Those rooms sound really cute – wallpaper and antique bedsteads – I love it! We'll leave them and get mattresses and box springs. I'll look around for some chenille bedspreads and rag rugs, and we'll be all set."

"I knew you would be able to do something with them."

*****

Peggy and Jeff decided to buy the house, sight unseen, and they signed the contract when they went to the Cape for Thanksgiving. This time they drove because they wanted the convenience of having their own car. Because there were so many things to do at the new house, they decided to stay at the Cape until after Christmas. The house was built in the 1920's, and it needed a lot of work. But it was on the ocean and the price was reasonable. Peggy commented, "When walking up to it, you would think, "What's the big deal?" But when you saw the sunset from the front windows, you thought you were in heaven."

Jeff knew the cost of renovation would more than double the value of the property. "We can't pass this up, Peggy, if we want beach front property, this may be our last opportunity at a reasonable price." As more and more people discovered the unhurried, peaceful, tranquil life on the Cape, prices would skyrocket, especially oceanfront property.

"I agree, Jeff, let's take it. I love the location; it's close to Mom and Dad and not far from Charlie and Lisa."

They hired a carpenter to convert the pantry to a powder room, and they hired a painter to remove the wallpaper and paint the great room white, and repaint the other rooms, including the kitchen, to give the house a fresh look. They shopped for furniture and other necessities, and they helped Jennie and Tom get ready for the Thanksgiving feast.

On Thanksgiving eve, Jennie and Tom, Charlie, Lisa and Sara, and Peggy and Jeff drove to Provincetown for the annual lighting of the Pilgrim Monument which celebrates the Pilgrim's first landing on November 11, 1620. It is one of Cape Cod's most beautiful traditions, and each couple donated $20.00 to support the traditional lighting. They felt it was something they would continue to attend and support each year. Afterward they stopped at the Lobster Pot café for soup and sandwiches. The soup of the day was lobster bisque, and as Lisa said, "it was to die for."

While at the café, Peggy and Jeff broke the news, with Jeff blurting out, "We're going to have a baby, and it was made in China." Of course, everyone laughed and joked about the China bit.

Lisa asked Peggy how far along she was and Peggy told her two months.

"You must be very excited," Lisa commented.

"Yes, we are excited, and the whole thing is really amazing. Well almost, until I feel nauseated."

"That will come and go, and then you'll feel wonderful," Jennie said. "Just keep a supply of soda crackers on hand."

"I've been busy decorating the nursery," Peggy said. "Right now it looks like a baby's playroom. Jeff gets carried away with stuffed animals."

Peggy continued, "When we were in China, we learned some of their traditions, and we were told that red-dyed eggs are given as birth announcements."

"What's the significance of that?" Tom asked.

"Eggs represent fertility and red symbolizes good luck. The eggs are given at the baby's one-month birthday since the baby is likely to survive if it reaches one month of age."

"That's because infant mortality rates in ancient China were quite high. Evidently it has become a part of their culture, and they continue the tradition today," Charlie said.

"Something else we learned – a baby's first birthday is celebrated with gifts of gold," Jeff said.

"Oh sure, they're the world leader in gold processing," Tom replied.

Laughing, Jeff replied, "We'll accept any gifts of gold."

Charlie chided Jeff, saying "Your baby will be born with the proverbial gold spoon…"

"I hope so, but with the liberals back in office, anything could happen." Jeff replied.

"Give him a chance; he hasn't even been inaugurated yet," Tom chimed in

Sensing two different political affiliations, Jennie said, "Now, now, let's not talk politics."

Charlie winked at Jeff and said, "Mother dislikes dissention. When she orchestrates these family gatherings, she wants us to be one big, happy family."

*****

Jennie and Tom rose early, and Tom prepared the turkey and put it in the oven. It was a big one, a 25-pounder. They had all agreed that leftovers were the best part of the meal. As usual, Jennie made the dressing and the cranberry sauce and candied sweet potatoes. Canned products were not acceptable to her family!

Peggy peeled the potatoes, and Lisa cut up celery, carrots and pickles for the relish tray. After a show of hands, corn was the winner for the vegetable.

Tom, Charlie and Jeff walked down to the beach for some fresh air. It was a bright sunny day, but the air felt cool. The sea was churning up spray and above there were a number of large white birds constantly turning and diving for fish.

"Sea gulls?" Jeff asked.

"No, those are Gannets. They are on their way to feeding grounds in the Caribbean. They hunt for fish in shallow waters. They won't stay around here long."

When they returned, they were greeted by the aroma of turkey and dressing, and Tom knew it was time to begin carving the turkey. He liked to carve it in the kitchen so it would be ready to pass around. With so many hands, dinner was ready to be served. Charlie poured the wine, Tom said Grace, and then the passing began. Lisa had fixed Sara's plate in the kitchen, and Sara was already well into her food, the mashed potatoes and gravy being the first to go.

"What's for dessert?" Charlie asked.

"We have pumpkin and apple pie," Jennie replied.

"I asked because if I didn't care for dessert, I'd eat more turkey and dressing. It's outstanding."

When everyone had their fill, they took their coffee to the great room to relax before going out for a walk down the beach. Tom related an incident that happened just recently:

"One night, we had a terrible storm with 40 to 50 mph winds and rain. There was thick fog, and the Coast Guard had received a distress signal from a fishing boat. Just before dawn they found an eighty-three foot trawler that had run aground on a sandbar. Huge beams of light swung out over the angry sea from a lighthouse, and fog horns groaned through the darkness, but it was too late, the ship was battered and beaten apart. Seven men were on board. Two Coast Guardsmen in a jeep had seen the wreck, and they rushed down to the shore. Some nearby residents also heard the commotion and rushed to the shore. Forming a hand-to-hand chain, the six rescuers managed by standing out far enough in the icy water to pull four men in. More Coast Guardsmen arrived and rescued two more. The survivors were numb from the cold and had to be forced into walking to save their lives. They kept mumbling as they stumbled around in the sand, "How much further?" Their skin was black and blue from the pounding they had taken from the surf. The other crewman was later found dead on the beach."

One woman bystander said, "I'll never complain about the price of fish again."

The boat, which was returning to Boston, had been carrying 38,000 pounds of fish. The fish were scattered by the surf and lying around, all for free, but not a single one was taken away."

"I didn't realize fishing could be so perilous. I'm surprised they were traveling at night," Jeff said.

"Oh, they do that all the time. They rely on the lighthouses and fog horns for direction, but they can't detect sand bars." Charlie replied.

"The wreck wasn't far from here, but we didn't know about it until morning," Tom said.

"And that was a good thing, he would have been down there wanting to help with the rescue," Jennie said.

*****

The following day they again drove to Provincetown as they had noticed 50% off sale signs in several stores on Commercial Street, and Jennie, Lisa and Peggy were anxious to find out what they had to offer. To their dismay, the sale signs were at the souvenir shops trying to unload an over stock of merchandise left over from the tourist season. They walked by kite stores, used bookstores, T-shirt shops, and boutiques where they sold cowry shells, dried starfish by the scoop, and sea glass by the pound. Jewelry stores displayed sea glass pendants and gold-dipped sand dollars. Peggy bought several shells and some sea glass for decoration, and Lisa bought glass pendants and sand dollars to make jewelry. The guys browsed the book store, and they each bought some books.

They walked past pizza parlors like the ones on every Main Street and a ramshackle clam shack that no outsider would think of entering but that served steaming platters of the best mussels you would ever hope to eat. It was so busy there was always a line waiting. Word got around fast.

"All summer this street is teeming with people. Ptown, as Providencetown is called, is the most popular town on the Cape," Charlie said.

"Lisa, would you and Charlie like to see the house we bought?" Peggy asked.

"Yes, we'd love to; we were just waiting for the right time to ask."

"Well, if we've seen everything here, let's go back to Barnstable and go through the house," Peggy replied.

When they neared the house and drove into the driveway, Lisa remarked, "I've seen this house before, and I wondered what it looked like inside.

It's so "cottagy" on the outside." As they toured the house, Peggy and Jeff told them what changes would be made to each room, the color scheme, etc. "Starting Monday, there will be workmen here for two weeks. We're going to be shopping for furniture, linens, pots and pans, everything we'll need to live here. We'd like to be able to live here for awhile before Christmas because we'll be leaving right after. In fact, Jeff and I would like to have everyone here Christmas Eve. I think we should take turns. Mom and Dad had Thanksgiving, and you and Charlie are doing Christmas dinner, so Christmas Eve will be our treat," Peggy said.

*****

It was two weeks before Christmas, and Peggy and Jeff were still living with Jennie and Tom. They were waiting for the box springs and mattresses to be delivered. Tom had started to cook dinner, when a dry snow shower began with swirls of snow flakes falling against the windows. Normally, Decembers were comparatively mild with sunshine and cool temperatures, but the temperature had plunged, and the weather bureau said the cold was the result of a Canadian high pressure system that was moving onto the Cape.

The snow continued to fall while they ate dinner, and a forecaster on the radio predicted they would have six to eight inches. It continued to snow through the evening. They watched the snow accumulate in between watching TV and going to the windows to watch the waves rolling onto the snow-covered beach. Before they turned the TV off to go to bed a forecast flashed across the bottom of the screen saying they now predicted ten to twelve inches. Tom groaned, he didn't even have a shovel, and the snow would have to be cleared from the driveway before they could get out.

"I guess we'll need to get a snow blower," Jeff said.

"Yes, we should at least have a shovel if we plan to be here in December." Tom replied.

It continued to snow throughout the night. In the morning Jennie walked to the window and wiped away the condensation. The snow was indeed thick, and she could see that the frontage road hadn't been plowed.

"We'll have to hire someone to plow out the driveway for us." Jennie said.

"Every plow in the county will be busy for days," Tom replied.

"Well, we don't have to go anyplace right away, so let's wait it out."

Throughout the day the snow fell steadily. At times the wind whistled and howled, but then it subsided as if it was giving up its attempt to become a blizzard. While Tom checked the phone directory for snow plowing services, Jennie went from room to room looking out the windows, crossing her arms, uncrossing them, and then wandering upstairs to stand at those windows and stare out."

"It isn't going to do any good to pace the floor, let's have some coffee and play some Scrabble," Tom said.

She went to the kitchen to make a pot of coffee and noticed through the window over the sink that it had stopped snowing. She let out a yell to Tom and went to the back door and opened it. She was immediately hit with a shower of fine powder that fell from the eave over the door. It appeared that there was much more than the predicted twelve inches.

The sun came out, and the snow outside was so bright they had to squint to look in the distance. Jeff and Peggy went to the front windows looking for signs of life. Tom joined them, and suddenly he cried out, "Hey, look, there's a snow plow coming down the frontage road." They continued to stand and watch, and the plow turned and came up their driveway.

"Well, isn't that great! That is wonderful," Tom said.

He put on his coat and went to the back door to talk to the driver when he finished plowing the driveway.

"Thanks a lot; you are a life-saver. How much do I owe you?"

"Not a dime. When we get an unusual snowstorm like this we automatically plow the drives when we are plowing the streets. This was a bad storm, more snow than I've ever seen here. This is very unusual."

Tom thanked him again and came inside.

"Wouldn't you know it! We decided to stay off-season, and we have the snowstorm of the century!" He said.

"It's our indoctrination. Now we know that it can happen. If it had to happen I'm glad it happened now so it wouldn't interrupt our Christmas plans. At least we'll have a white Christmas. Best of all, we'll all be together, that's what matters," she said.

In between shopping trips to furnish the house and oversee the renovation, Peggy, Jeff, Jennie and Tom took advantage of the special holiday events that took place in the various communities. The Holly Festival in Ptown, the holiday pops concert in Barnstable, and the Falmouth Christmas parade were gatherings they didn't want to miss.

*****

On Christmas Eve after Charlie, Lisa and Sara had arrived, they went to the same white clapboard Congregational church with long windows and black shutters, its tall white steeple a beacon to returning fishermen. A light snow was falling, and the church was warm and inviting. They made their way to the front pews and relaxed in the calmness that spread throughout the church. The Christmas Eve 5 p.m. candlelight service was always packed. Where forty attended church on Sundays, Christmas Eve drew two hundred. The Fire Chief had sent his usual letter warning about open flames in the church. But the deacons said, "We haven't burned this place down in two hundred years." So the tradition continued.

After the service, Peggy and Jeff led the way to their new home where they would enjoy wine and appetizers followed by steaming bowls of lobster bisque from the Lobster Pot. They were noted for their bisque, and Peggy had put in their order a week in advance. After supper, they would open their presents.

As they drove through town they passed houses where strings of colored lights hung from the eaves and lighted Christmas trees shone through the front windows. The house next to theirs was a blue-shingled Cape with an outline of gaudy colored bulbs surrounding the front window.

"You'll never see that at our house," Peggy commented.

Lisa and Charlie hadn't seen Peggy and Jeff's newly decorated home, and Peggy led them on a tour. They gasped at seeing the great room with white painted walls and splashes of turquoise and sea green throughout which brought the seascape indoors for a beachy look. A lime wash on the wide plank oak floors mimicked the sandy beach. In lieu of a Christmas tree the antique brick fireplace mantle was laden with greens and gold and silver ornaments. Sea shells decorated tables, and the sea glass that Peggy bought in Ptown filled clear glass jars on the coffee table. Furniture in navy and white completed the nautical décor.

"You'll note that we brought the sea into almost every room by using aqua, turquoise and navy in the color scheme," Peggy stated.

"Yes, and I love it, it's like endless ocean views," Lisa replied.

"Its going to be difficult to leave this place and go back to Chicago," Jeff said, "But we do have wonderful views of Lake Michigan from almost every room."

"We're looking forward to seeing your penthouse apartment," Charlie stated, "We hope to get back there next year."

While they were enjoying wine and appetizers the conversation turned to Peggy's pregnancy.

"Do you have names picked out for the baby?" Lisa asked.

"Since Jeff refers to the baby as my son or our son, we have selected Thomas Martin Burnham for a boy's name," Peggy replied. "If it should happen to be a girl, I like the name, Margaret, and we would call her Margie or Maggie."

"Those are pretty names," Jennie said.

"I'm honored that you are going to name your son, Thomas, I hope he will like it as I have," Tom said.

"I forgot to tell you that it will be a C-section baby. I was told that my pelvic structure is too small to have a vaginal birth," Peggy said.

"There's nothing wrong with that, it happens a lot. The bad part is the recovery is longer," Jennie stated. "Its major surgery; and you have to be careful of lifting and stairs."

"My doctor said it will take four weeks before I'm free of pain and can walk for a distance, but he said every person is different, some women take longer, some less." Peggy replied.

They were interrupted by the loud bawl of a foghorn, and they knew there was a ship that was possibly lost and unknown. They rushed to the window. Even though it was dark they could see and hear the ocean's swells and breakers as they crashed onto the shore. Suddenly there was a tremendous thud above that jarred and shook the house.

"It's a plane breaking the sound barrier," Charlie cried out.

They stood motionless at the window and a minute or two later they heard the familiar honking of geese, and they pictured a large flock of geese frightened by the noise of the plane fleeing their feeding grounds along the shores of Cape Cod Bay.

Then there was almost complete silence again, and they moved back into the room.

"Let's have supper, and then we'll open presents," Peggy said. They all gathered around the table enjoying their lobster bisque, garlic toast, and lemon cheesecake for dessert.

"I'm glad we found a house on the seashore; there's always something amazing going on." Jeff said.

As they were saying good-night, Jeff told Jennie and Tom they would pick them up tomorrow. "There's no use both of us driving." He asked Charlie, "What time shall we come?"

"Come about eleven, we have a surprise for you," Charlie replied.

Christmas day was a brilliantly sunny day, but the air was cool. The shore was desolate except for gulls drifting slowly over the beach in search of food brought ashore by the constant plunging and spraying of the waves at the shore.

Jeff and Peggy picked up Jennie and Tom, and they had barely knocked on Charlie's door when they were greeted by the cutest golden lab puppy standing there barking and jumping up and down. A red Christmas bow was tied around its neck, and in a moment Sara was saying, "It' all right, Sam."

Charlie and Lisa were beaming with happiness saying, "What do you think? Isn't he just like Sam?"

Charlie continued, "I saw him in the window of a pet shop, and I couldn't walk away. I've never forgotten Sam, and now its like he has always been a part of our lives. Sara loves him, and he loves her."

Lisa added, "Now I realize that Sara needed a puppy. She's a much happier child. She's less dependent on us for attention; she thinks she needs to take care of Sam. She will be less spoiled as a result."

Sara sprawled with Sam on the rug, and she wrapped her arms around him, hugging him to her. "You good puppy," she told him, and he licked her face, delirious with love.

"I'm so glad you found him," Jennie said. "He's just like our Sam, and he will be a good protector and companion to Sara."

Tom reached out to pet Sam, and he felt him quiver. "Steady now, Sam, everything's going to be fine." Sam let Tom stroke him and rough his fur. Sam immediately licked his hand, and they both knew there would always be a bond between them.

"This is a wonderful surprise. Now Sara can grow up with him. I was too young to realize what happened to our Sam, but I knew for a long time that Charlie missed him." Peggy said.

"Yes, I did, and I knew another dog couldn't take his place then because we were too overcome with grief. But now that time has passed, I can look at this little guy who is the spitting image of him and just love him for who he is."

"Do you want to eat now or after the game?" Charlie asked. "We have lots of nibblies."

"After, please. What are we having?" Tom asked.

"We're having a traditional southern cured ham." Lisa replied.

The New York Giants were playing the Green Bay Packers, and they knew it would be a close and exciting game. Tom and Jeff were Packer fans, and Charlie would root for his hometown Giants. Fresh snow covered the town of Green Bay, but the field had been covered with a tarp so it was spotless. The Giant players wore long-sleeved jerseys, but as usual the Packers toughed it in short-sleeved jerseys.

The teams were closely matched, and the first quarter was scoreless but that quickly changed. In the second quarter the Packer's quarterback made an 8-yard touchdown pass to make it 7-0.

During half-time they went out on the porch for some fresh air and replenished their drinks.

The third quarter was scoreless. Then the Packers scored late in the fourth quarter when a player carried the ball into the end zone on a two-yard touchdown run to end the game at 14-0. The fans went wild.

Tom and Jeff high-fived, and Charlie said "Wait until next year…"

Chapter Twenty-Two

Jeff and Peggy were often seen making their way along Water Street in the yellow Mercedes. Jeff was busy with his latest real estate venture. He had purchased an old 6-six-story brick warehouse on Water Street near Lake Michigan, and he was going to rehab it into loft apartments similar to the TriBeCa lofts in New York City. He had to get his architectural plans approved by City Planning, and the Building Department had to approve the electrical plans. Even the Landmarks Preservation Commission had to approve the plans.

He had a lot of time and money invested in blueprints, building permits, and attorney's fees, and he wanted everything to be approved without having to redo anything. His father had previously worked with the city bureaucrats and made friends, or greased their palms as so often was the case when dealing with city bureaucrats, so Jeff thought it would be easier for him to go through the city regulatory departments. "I hope we won't have to refigure our cost figures," he told Peggy. "We can't afford to lose money on this project."

Peggy was past the nauseous stage of her pregnancy, and she was feeling great. She had collaborated with Jeff on the architectural plans so she had a vested interest in the project. They were a husband-wife team, and they both were involved in overseeing the project from beginning to end. When Jeff wasn't available to answer a question or comment on the plans, Peggy stepped in for him.

They planned to create upscale loft apartments with an artistic flare, incorporating giant picture windows, exposed pipes, and distressed beams. The artist-loft concept was very popular with young professionals. The building would be converted into twelve lofts (with two penthouse units), and they would be priced at just under $2.5 million. They wanted to rehab the building, sell off the apartments, and move on. They didn't want to become landlords. They knew buyers would be willing to pay a relatively steep price to live in that neighborhood and have a view of Lake Michigan from almost every window.

They would call the building "The Lofts on Water Street." With the revitalization of Water Street, it was now becoming a swanky address. The grand old buildings that had been neglected and had become obsolete were now being replaced by attractive apartments and upscale retail shops. When Jeff and Peggy were interviewed by a reporter for a newspaper article, Peggy commented, "Instead of being drab and broken down, it's going to look alive and inviting. It will be a wonderful addition to the lakefront." Jeff commented, "The project doesn't revolve around profit, but around restoring the beauty of the lakefront. We want to bring a 95-year old building back to life."

The project energized them, and they couldn't have been happier. They breezed through January and February oblivious to Chicago's cold, drab weather. Peggy was going into her seventh month, and her doctor was pleased with her health. He assured her she would have a normal cesarean delivery and a healthy baby. She asked him if it was still safe to have sex, and he replied, "Oh, yes, its safe right up to delivery." He also told her she was carrying the baby very low which indicated the baby would probably be a boy.

When she arrived home, Jeff asked about her examination and what the doctor had to say. "He said it's safe to have sex, and its going to be a boy." Jeff smiled and said, "That's just what I wanted to hear."

"Mom has invited us over for dinner so we should leave now."

"That's a nice surprise, I'm ready."

Of course, the conversation turned to the apartment project, and Jeff told them, "Everything has been approved, and we've started with construction."

"Do you think they'll sell well? What's the market like?" Tom asked.

"Lofts are hot right now, and we are already getting calls. People are looking for these types of apartments, and they don't want to rent them, they want to buy." Jeff replied.

"I'm sure the location is a bonus," Jennie commented.

"Yes, Water Street is a classy address now," Peggy said.

"When are you planning to go to the Cape? Jennie asked.

"In July, for the fourth. The baby will be two months old then. When will you be going?" Peggy asked.

"We'll leave shortly after the baby is born. We don't want to miss seeing him for the first time."

"It's funny you should say "him." Just today the doctor told me it would probably be a boy because I'm carrying it low."

Jennie offhandedly said, "Well, I suppose the reason I said "him" is because Jeff insists he is going to have a son." She stated further, "Charlie and Lisa plan to be there for the 4th too."

"Barnstable puts on a glorious fireworks display, and we'll watch it from the beach. Tom and Charlie plan to build a bonfire, and we'll roast wieners and make s'mores," Jennie added.

"That sounds fun," Peggy replied. "Jeff wants to get a surfboard and go surfing. He's never done it before. He thinks that if you live on the ocean, you have to be a surfer."

"We don't get the giant waves there, but he'd still have fun," Jennie replied.

"Let's spend the day at our place, it will make things easier with a small baby," Peggy said.

"Yes, it would be more convenient for you and Jeff. Charlie and Lisa suggested that we be at their place because of the dog, but I'm sure they'll understand. They can bring Sam along."

When Peggy was going into her ninth month, for the first time in her pregnancy she was becoming depressed and irritable. Her stomach had gotten larger and because she was carrying the baby low, it was an effort to even walk. Beth came often to keep her company. Beth was anxious to have a grandchild, and she wanted what every mother wants for her children, to raise a family and have a long and happy life together. She knew that Jeff and Peggy would be wonderful parents, they were madly in love and devoted to each other, and they wanted a child more than anything.

The day before Peggy was scheduled for delivery, Beth stopped by. She looked very attractive in white pants and a chocolate-brown Armani sweater, and Peggy wondered if she would ever lose her weight and once again be attractive.

Beth asked, "Would you like me to help you after you get home from the hospital?"

"Oh, would you please, Beth. I hesitated to ask you. Mom and Dad are leaving for the Cape right after the baby is born."

"Of course I will. That's what grandmothers are for."

"Are you going to nurse?" Beth asked.

"Yes, Dr. Feldman recommended it. He said the baby will be healthier."

"He's right!"

Jeff entered the room and first kissed Peggy and then his mother, asking "and how are my two favorite women?"

"What time are we due at the hospital tomorrow?" he asked Peggy.

"The C-section is scheduled for nine, and I have to be there two hours before, so I should be there at seven."

Peggy had everything memorized. Fast tonight, nothing to eat or drink eight hours before surgery not even water. Arrive two hours early for pre-surgery preparation such as shaving the incision site, blood tests, meeting with the anesthesiologist, and insertion of catheter. She had been preparing for this day. She wanted to see their baby, count his toes and fingers, look into his eyes, and hold him. She wondered what Jeff's reaction would be. Dr. Feldman assured her that everything would go smoothly.

She knew she would be in the hospital three or four days after delivery, and she was happy that Beth would be with her at home.

While Peggy was in the recovery room, a blue-and-white wrapped bundle was put in her arms. Dr. Feldman told her he weighed 7 lbs, 6 ozs, and he was a completely healthy baby. He had brown hair and blue eyes, and his fingers opened and closed like they were supposed to. She thought he was the most beautiful baby she had ever seen. She bounced him lightly in her arms and cuddled him close to her chest.

When she left recovery and was wheeled to her private room, Jeff was there waiting. He kissed her and looked at the baby in her arms. "Hi," he said softly, and the baby focused his eyes on him.

"Want to hold him?" Peggy asked.

"Is it okay?" he asked.

"Sure," she said and carefully placed the baby in his arms.

Jeff stared at him in silence, and Peggy asked, "Are you all right?"

"Fine," he said quietly. "He's beautiful, and he's ours."

Jeff gave him his pinkie finger to grab, and he took it and held it tight.

"He's strong, he doesn't want to let go."

"He wants you to stay," Peggy remarked.

"I won't ever leave you, Tommy," Jeff whispered to him.

*****

Peggy was sore and tired the first week at home, but then she was eager to go shopping, have lunch, and be out and about.

When Beth saw Tommy, she exclaimed, "He's the perfect image of Jeff when he was born!"

"I think he looks like Jeff, too. The doctor said he's going to be tall, he's 22 inches long." Peggy said.

Jennie and Tom couldn't have been happier. Now they had a grandson. What they wanted most was a healthy and happy family.

Jeff told them that having a baby was like falling in love again. Peggy remarked, "Jeff is the perfect father, he's so caring."

She mentioned to Beth, "I remember when we were in China, we saw many women walking around carrying their babies in slings with the baby nestled to their chests. Their hands were free to do whatever needed to be done. I'm going to get a baby sling. It would be great for shopping."

They took advantage of Beth's stay and went to a favorite restaurant in downtown Chicago for dinner. Peggy was dressed in an elegant black slim dress with black heels, and she was gorgeous. Jeff ordered a bottle of wine, and they both ordered Dover sole.

He raised his glass in a toast, and said, "Here's to our success as real estate developers, and to Peggy Burnham's success as an architect." Jeff had told her the last unsold apartment was sold, and they made more money on the project than originally estimated.

They both sat back and laughed. Peggy raised her hand, and Jeff high-fived her.

"I've decided to look for another building to rehab. We'll become a team and call ourselves, "Burnham Ventures."

"It might not be so easy. Location is everything in the real estate business," Peggy replied.

"That's true; those apartments sold well because of the lakefront location," Jeff said.

"We'll need to find something that has a special "draw" to it," she said.

"Yes, even if we have to go away from the lakefront area."

"What about the Cape?" Peggy asked.

"I'd rather stay in the Chicago area, but let's look around while we're there this summer," Jeff said.

*****

Early in the morning on April 1st, Peggy and Jeff loaded their new black Land Rover Defender and left for the Cape. The Land Rover was acquired just before Tommy came into their world.

"We'll need a large vehicle to transport us and the baby's stuff back and forth from the Cape," Jeff reasoned.

Boxes, luggage, the baby's crib and a bicycle secured with bungees were packed in the back of the vehicle and a canary yellow surfboard was stowed on the roof rack. It would be a two-day drive to celebrate the 4th of July on the Cape.

The morning of the 4th was hot and humid, and the beach was already getting crowded. Soon it would be filled with bodies, lying everywhere, or sitting, talking, absorbing the sun and suddenly dashing into the water, shouting, jumping and splashing, then returning to the ritual of doing nothing. No one owns the beach so like everyone else Charlie, Tom and Jeff took their umbrellas, beach balls, and towels down to the beach to stake out their location in the sand.

"Want to come?" Charlie asked as he picked up the red leash. Sam ran in circles jumping up and down in excitement acting as though he had been imprisoned for weeks.

"Stay," Charlie said, struggling to snag the collar so he could fasten the clip, but Sam wouldn't be still.

"You have to wonder how smart he is," Charlie said. "He wants to go for a walk more than anything in the world, and he knows we can't go for a walk until the leash is on, but he won't let me put it on him!"

"Does he need a leash here?" Jeff asked.

"Yes, he'd run into the water and try to chase gulls, and we wouldn't see him again for hours. I'll remove the leash later when he's tired."

They crossed the frontage road to the beach, carrying their surfboards with the slap of their flip-flops echoing as they walked.

Peggy was wearing a white one-piece bathing suit that showed off her new trim figure, and her skin glistened from sunscreen oil. She was carrying Tommy who was wearing a blue sun suit, and she carefully put him on a beach towel underneath a beach umbrella. Jennie, Lisa, and Sara spread their beach towels around him.

"You look fantastic in that suit," Jeff remarked.

"Thanks. You look good, too," Peggy said. He was wearing knee-length shorts in a navy and white floral pattern.

While the water was flat or the waves were really small, Jeff and Charlie got a kick out of stand-up paddle surfing. When knee high or waist high waves rolled in they picked up their boards and raced to ride them to the shore. It seemed the waves were a living thing that had no purpose but to carry them along at a tremendous speed. Jeff was thrilled with his new sport and didn't want to stop. They rode a third wave and then a fourth. He had never felt so exhilarated.

"My god," he said wiping the water from his eyes.

"You okay?" Charlie asked.

"That was unbelievable."

He listened for the next swell coming in with a roar. He felt intoxicated with excitement as he rode the wave into the shore. Then he stood and waded out again with his yellow surfboard as a huge wall of water was rolling in. Peggy watched him as he ran forward to meet the ocean. He tried to ride the wave to the shore, but he got yanked into the ocean's grasp. Peggy didn't know it at the time, but Jeff had been pulled in by the riptide.

Charlie saw the situation and rushed to the water. He dove into the strong wave and "porpoised" through, a trick he had learned in college. He heard Peggy's shrieking voice pleading, "Please help Jeff." The strong currents kept pushing him back as he again and again used his porpoise technique to break through.

It was horrible seeing the trouble he was in and not being able to communicate with him or help him. Someone had alerted the beach patrol, and they hurried to try to find him, but they were not able to locate him.

A small crowd of sunbathers formed around Peggy, their faces dumbstruck. As the word "riptide" was whispered, knowing the outcome, they slowly and silently dispersed.

On the verge of collapse, Charlie managed to make it back to shore. He had to crawl out of the water. Lisa was frantic. He struggled to get his breath. There was water in his mouth and nose. He had swallowed a lot of salt water and was vomiting.

Tom wanted to take him to the hospital, but he refused.

A Coast Guard officer arrived, and he tried to console Peggy who was trembling and crying loudly. He told her they were searching for his body, and he would keep her informed. He gave her his card and told her she could call him any time.

Peggy was panic-stricken. She wouldn't leave the beach thinking that at any time Jeff's body would be washed ashore. It was the middle of the night, and they couldn't see the water, but she stood there crying. Jennie and Lisa had taken the children back to the house, and Tom and Charlie stayed trying to console her and persuading her to leave and go indoors.

When they finally convinced her that she should leave the beach and come inside, she picked up the phone and called Beth. It was one o'clock in the morning, but she had to talk to her. Beth was stunned at the news, and she cried uncontrollably. Peggy tried to convince her that he would still be found, but they both knew it wasn't true. Peggy told her they would return to Chicago as soon as they received final word from the Coast Guard, and they would make plans for a memorial service.

Then she thought, if you had a memorial service, was it best to have it right away, or wait a bit? What happened if you had a memorial service and then, a week later, the body was found. Then should you have a funeral? She hoped that the service would bring a kind of closure, but then she didn't want closure, she wanted to keep his memory alive forever.

The next morning before daybreak Peggy went back and walked up and down the beach, a distance of two miles. Jeff's surfboard had washed ashore, but there was no sign of his body. She picked up the surfboard and brought it back to the house. She didn't yet know whether she wanted it around as a reminder.

She heard Tommy fussing and went to his room. When she stood over his crib to lift him, he waved his arms and smiled at her. She picked him up and cuddled him to her. He was all she had now. After she had bathed and fed him, she put him in his play pen with some toys to play with.

She looked over at the shirt that Jeff had flung on a chair before he went to the beach, and tears welled in her eyes. She didn't want to remove it; it would be days before she could touch it or risk bringing it to her face to catch his smell on the cloth. Everywhere she looked, he was there, in every chair, in every room. When all traces of him were put away, what would she be left with? She couldn't bear to part with anything.

She went to the window and gazed down at the beach. A jeep stopped and some teen-aged boys jumped out carrying their boogie boards. A wave advanced, and they ran to the water. Peggy could hear its anger. She turned away from the window.

Jennie and Tom came to be with her and to help her get through the saddest and most trying days of her life. Peggy picked up the card which read, "Commander Rene Goddard, U.S. Coast Guard, Rescue Operations, Barnstable, Mass."

"Shall I call him now?"

Then there was a knock at the door. The Coast Guard officer introduced himself as Rene Goddard. He was tall with hazel eyes and the hair that was visible beneath his uniform cap was brown. He had an accent, French maybe.

Peggy started to cry, and the officer put his arm around her shoulder and told her he was very sorry.

"Our helicopters have spent hours searching the waters without success. A helicopter pilot has been scouring the shore up and down the Cape. We have found nothing. We will continue to search for your husband's body, but I did want to inform you that we do not hold any hope of finding him. You may want to proceed with the necessary arrangements. Again, I'm very sorry, Mrs. Burnham, but please do not hesitate to call me if I can be of service to you."

Tom spoke up and asked, "What will we do for a death certificate?"

Mr. Goddard told them that the Coast Guard would issue a statement that would suffice as a death certificate after they had completed their search efforts.

"When will that be?" Jennie asked.

"We'll continue to search through the rest of the week, and if nothing is found, we will, of course, have to end our rescue efforts and a statement will be issued at that time."

Peggy began to cry and stated, "I'm never going to leave here. What if his body would wash ashore?"

Jennie and Tom put their arms around Peggy and thanked the officer for coming.

At the end of the week, Rene Goddard returned with a statement regarding Jeff's disappearance. It read:

"In July of 1995, the Barnstable, Mass. U.S. Coast Guard Rescue Operations conducted the largest search and rescue mission for a single man, and the body of Jeffrey Burnham was never found. He was lost at sea."

Peggy's heart sank and her hand shook as she read the statement. She had never given up hope of finding his body, and she couldn't believe what she was reading.

As they were preparing to leave, Peggy began to cry, "We bought this house for the idea of family. We imagined it would be a place where our family would gather every summer. We wanted the beach, the water… I loved him."

Jennie put her arm around her. "Tom and I loved him, too. We all loved him."

Jennie and Tom rode with Peggy in her Land Rover, and Charlie, Lisa, Sara and Sam drove separately.

*****

The headline of the Chicago Tribune read: "Chicago Businessman Lost at Sea." The Chicago Sun-Times' headline read, "Millionaire Lost at Sea."

A memorial service was held at the First Presbyterian Church in Lincoln Park where they were married. Peggy and Beth, Jennie and Tom, all dressed in black, greeted the guests as they arrived for the service. Close friends like Suzanne and Matt Shapiro and Lauren and Peter Adler hugged them desperately.

A soloist from the church sang "Amazing Grace", and a childhood friend of Jeff's recited W. H. Auden's poem, "Funeral Blues." There was complete silence, no clearing of throats or rustling of paper. Some silently wiped away tears.

Funeral Blues

Stop all the clocks, cut off the telephone,
Prevent the dog from barking with a juicy bone,
Silence the pianos and with muffled drum
Bring out the coffin, let the mourners come.

Let aeroplanes circle moaning overhead
Scribbling on the sky the message 'He is Dead.'
Put crepe bows round the white necks of the public doves, Let the traffic policemen wear black cotton gloves.

He was my North, my South, my East and West,
My working week and my Sunday rest,
My noon, my midnight, my talk, my song;
I thought that love would last forever: I was wrong.

The stars are not wanted now; put out every one,
Pack up the moon and dismantle the sun,
Pour away the ocean and sweep up the wood;
For nothing now can ever come to any good.

W.H. Auden

Then the minister spoke, and he asked the audience to feel free to say a few words about the deceased.

Tom stated, "Our family finds some solace in the fact that he died doing something he loved."

"Jeff had absolutely no fear, and he loved being in the ocean. He absolutely loved the ocean," Jennie said.

Charlie said, "He was doing what he wanted to do and where he wanted to do it."

"He could fit more in a day than most people I know, and there was so much more that he planned to do. It's a very sad thing," Beth commented.

Peggy said, "He was incredibly vibrant, and he loved being out there at the beach."

Many of his friends were in such shock that they couldn't speak, but a manager at Burnham Electric said, "He was one of my favorite people, he was down to earth, caring, intelligent, fun to be with."

Peggy managed to keep her composure throughout the service, until the soloist ended the service by singing "I'll Always Love You." Most everyone in the audience wept with her.

After the service, everyone was invited for lunch at a nearby restaurant, but most people left to go back to their work, or their day. The dining room filled with close friends and family. They wanted to show Peggy that they cared.

The following day, Beth accompanied Peggy when she met with their lawyer. They were not surprised to learn that Jeff had taken care of their estate and everything was in order. Even Beth's home in Lake Forest would become hers in time, and the high-rise apartment building where she lived was all hers. The profit on the sale of the Lofts was substantial. Peggy was a multi-millionaire and worth more money than she had ever dreamed possible. She and Jeff hadn't discussed their financial situation; there would always be time for that. She felt secure in knowing that they had a sufficient amount of money to live comfortably for the rest of their lives.

However, her sudden wealth was not without worry. Who would run Burnham Electric? Now she would have to learn the ins and outs of that business and select the best possible management team. Having money did not mean that she would be free of worries.

Charlie and Lisa had left to return to the Cape, and now Peggy with Tommy and Jennie and Tom were leaving. Inwardly, she thought Jeff's body would still wash ashore, and she needed to be there. But in another breath she told herself she would have to learn to live without him. All that she imagined that their life would be now will never happen, and she saw herself walking alone on city streets. It would be another existence. Isn't that what all widows do? What about Tommy? Becoming a single mother had never entered her mind. She was glad that he was too young to know. She wouldn't have to answer his childish questions – where's daddy? I want daddy!

After they arrived, she fed Tommy and put him in his crib. He closed his eyes in a deep sleep. She walked down to the beach, looking out across the ocean while the cool water rushed over her ankles. The beach looked different at night. The footprints had been erased as if nobody had ever set foot there. It was getting dark, and she thought of the times when they went to the beach after dark with blankets and beer, and swam naked in the cool moonlit water. She stood looking out at the black water and then slowly returned to the house.

She stood immobile in the shower, hoping the water would wash the world away so she wouldn't have to think and wonder. Then she dried her hair and slid between the sheets. This would be her bed now. Her bed alone. She rolled onto her side and looked toward the window. Through the opened window she could hear the water lapping at the shore. She closed her eyes, and she had a vision of Jeff in the water, being tossed about on the sand at the bottom of the ocean. She got up and went to the bathroom. Did she really imagine that she could spend this first night alone in their bed? She took a sleeping pill and went back to bed. Within seconds she fell asleep.

*****

Peggy walked blindly up and down the beach, her head down against the wind, her baby in a sling around her shoulder. Her hair was pulled back in a pony tail, and her face was tanned and weathered as if she spent most of her days in the sun. The noise of the waves splashing against the shore muffled his footsteps, and then she saw him coming toward her.

"Mrs. Burnham, is there anything I can do for you?" Rene asked, "I've seen you walking the beach almost every day."

"You can call me, Peggy. I want to be here in case my husband's body washes ashore. It will sometime, won't it?" Jeff's death left her in a state of emotional paralysis. She was unable to believe that Jeff was gone. If there wasn't a body, how could he be gone forever.

"The ocean is a vast expanse – endless. We don't expect that his body will ever wash ashore. You are tormenting yourself by walking the beach every day looking for his body. You look cold, can I buy you a cup of coffee or some hot chocolate? Let's go into town."

She was cold, and Tommy was stirring. "I'll make some coffee. The baby is waking, and he will be hungry. My house is up ahead."

He fell into step with her. "What is your baby's name?"

"It's Tommy. We named him after my father. His name is actually Thomas Martin Burnham. Martin was my husband's father's name."

"He looks like a very contented baby," He said.

"Sometimes I think that losing his father at this stage in his life was probably better than later, but he'll never know him, he'll always wonder what his father was like. His father will never see him grow up, become a teenager. There's no best time to lose a father. That's my house," and she pointed to it.

Peggy got the Mr. Coffee machine going, and then she excused herself and took Tommy to his room where she changed him and kissed him and put him in his crib. He smiled at her and then closed his eyes.

She poured two mugs of coffee and took them to the great room.

"Do you feel like talking about your husband?"

"He was not a person that got scared, and he was an excellent swimmer. That's what makes this so unreal. He was a fun-loving, thoughtful man, and we were very much in love."

"I'm sorry," he said and paused.

Before he could go on, Peggy said, "I'm tired of hearing people saying they're sorry."

"Some people find it difficult to console the grief-stricken. I'll try not to overuse those words. It's because I'm worried about you. I'd like to help you overcome your grief or be able to live with it, but I know it takes time for people to mend."

"Do they? Mend? She asked.

"Given enough time they do," he replied.

"I know, and I apologize for that remark. I do appreciate having someone to talk to."

Tommy began to cry, and Peggy excused herself. Rene said he had to leave and asked if he could come back some day. She told him she would like that and he left.

*****

Jennie and Tom also worried about Peggy. For her sake and Tommy's, they tried to get her engrossed in things that would ease her heartache.

"We'd like you to remember not just that he died, but that he lived, and that he gave you memories too beautiful to forget," Jennie said, and she continued, "The Barnstable Symphony Orchestra is having an outdoor concert in the city park tonight. They are going to celebrate Gershwin's amazing talent. Come with us, we are going to take blankets and supper. We'll spread out on the lawn like the Ravinia concerts in Chicago. It'll be fun."

"Mom, that does sound like fun. It would be good for Tommy, too. It's never too early to be exposed to music."

Along with their picnic hamper and blankets, they all piled in the Land Rover and drove to the park. Their impromptu little picnic included wine, cheese, bread and a lobster salad.

It had been a sunny clear blue sky day, but as they neared the park sullen gray clouds began to roll in. Oblivious to the sky, crowds of people entered the park and staked their claim on the lawn. The master of ceremonies glanced up at the dark clouds in the sky, and said, "They're just passing through. We have lots of good music for you tonight so just sit back and enjoy."

The orchestra began their repertoire with a rousing march from Strike up the Band and followed with "I Got Rhythm." A roll of thunder was heard in the distance, followed by a streak of lightning across the sky. They continued to play and soon rain drops were falling and the rumbling thunder came closer. Another streak of lightning lit up the sky, and the band stopped playing. The emcee returned and said, "We're very sorry folks, but we'll have to call it quits for tonight." Many people had already hurried to their cars, and Jennie and Tom hurriedly packed up the remains of their supper as the rain came down heavier. Tommy began to cry, and Peggy wrapped him in his blanket and hurried to the Land Rover.

"It's too bad they don't have a covered band shell or a pavilion like they have at Ravinia," Peggy said.

They probably can't afford it, Jennie said. "But I hope they reschedule the program for next week."

That night when Peggy was laying in bed her thoughts went back to the concert. She remembered her mother's remark that they probably couldn't afford to have a pavilion. In her mind she pictured a pavilion in the park and thought, "*that's what I'll do to honor Jeff. I'll design and build a pavilion in his name. I know he would want me to do something here at the Cape that would be a lasting memorial for future generations of "Cape Codders" and tourists to enjoy.*

The Cape was going to be his second home. He had fallen in love with the ocean and the beach. She winced as her thoughts included the ocean, but then she remembered him saying he would like to spend the rest of his life at the ocean." How ironic that those words would ring true.

The next morning she felt like a new person, like there was a purpose and a future to her life. She showered and went to the kitchen to start the coffee and then went to Tommy's room. He was smiling and waving his arms in the air as if he too had been energized. She scooped him up in her arms and hugged and kissed him. After she had bathed and fed him, she began sketching designs for a pavilion based upon her memory of the Ravinia pavilion in Chicago.

It would be an open-air design, covered pavilion, and it would overlook the ocean. It would offer shelter to the musicians or performers and about 200 people with seating on the lawn for those who wished to listen to the music while picnicking. The park wasn't large enough for a larger pavilion, but its size would be ample. The large stage area would have state-of the-art sound, video and lighting equipment. She would get cost estimates and donate the funds to have it built. It would be named the Jeffrey Burnham Pavilion, and it would be a gift to the city of Barnstable. She envisioned various performances from the symphony to rock bands being held every summer from June to September.

Peggy became so absorbed in the pavilion that she didn't have time to walk the beach every day to look for Jeff's body.

Late Sunday afternoon her doorbell rang, and Rene Goddard stood there smiling and holding a box of candy. He was out of uniform, wearing khaki shorts, a white cotton shirt, and sandals. His long legs were lean and tanned.

Handing her the candy, he said, "Let's go for a drive to Brewster."

"What's in Brewster on a Sunday?" Peggy asked.

"A wonderful seafood bar. I think you'll love it," he replied.

"I love seafood, come in, and I'll get Tommy ready."

As they were driving down the frontage road, Rene said "I haven't seen you on the beach lately."

"I've been very busy." And she eagerly told him about the pavilion project. "I haven't had time to think about anything else. I hope the city will approve and accept my donation."

"That's a wonderful and very generous thing for you to do. How can they not accept your fine gift!"

Rene thought to himself that this project was the best thing for her. She was relaxed, radiant, and cheerful, a far cry from the tense and despondent person she had been. With grief, he thought appearance was the first thing to go.

The seafood bar was noisy and crowded, but the aroma overshadowed everything around them. They ordered a glass of wine, clam chowder and a crusty loaf of bread. Peggy had brought a bottle of milk for Tommy, and he busied himself with that.

When they finished, Rene ordered lemon cheesecake and coffee saying, "No one walks out of here without tasting their cheesecake. It is superb," and on second thought, he asked, "do you like lemon?"

Actually, it's my favorite, how did you know?"

Peggy realized she knew very little about him, and she asked, "Your accent, is it French?"

"I'm Canadian, French Canadian. From Quebec. I've been here twelve years. He laughed and said he didn't realize he had an accent. He enlisted in the Coast Guard as soon as he became a citizen because he loves boats and the sea, and he likes search and rescue.

"Isn't it depressing to see so many people drown or lose their lives at sea?"

"Yes, it is, but saving a life more than makes up for it, and actually we don't lose many lives. Your husband was a very unusual case. How are you doing? Is it getting easier?"

"Yes, to have the pavilion exist as a memorial would bring the closure that I need. I can't cry anymore. That part is over. The pavilion would take the place of a tombstone. It's very difficult to not have anything to show that he existed, and I know Jeff would approve. He loved it here, and he wanted to spend the rest of his life at the ocean."

"You're doing the right thing – I think you are mending well. It's the perfect way to honor him, and it will be a lasting memorial for both you and Tommy. He'll need to have a remembrance of his father. I'm certain the city will be pleased with your gift."

*****

Peggy found a company in Boston that would build the pavilion to her design and specifications, and the City of Barnstable was extremely grateful for her wonderful gift, saying it would be a spectacular addition to the oceanfront. She wouldn't see it until next summer when there would be a ceremony to unveil the pavilion and honor Jeff.

It was October 1st, and she was preparing to return to Chicago. It was difficult to close up the house and leave. She had felt she was bound to the ocean to be near Jeff. They had made a vow to never part. Everything that was in store for him, she would never know.

Jennie would ride with her so they could take turns driving while she administered to Tommy's needs. The Land Rover was packed and ready for an early morning start.

Tommy had been cutting teeth for a week, and to ease his pain, she tried everything her mother had suggested from her experience. The teething ring gave some relief for about fifteen minutes. The Oragel that she rubbed onto his gums soothed him long enough to fall asleep for an hour. Then Lisa told her he would sleep through the night pain-free if she gave him an infant Tylenol before bed time. That is what she had done now while rocking him asleep in the rocking chair.

His warm little body was cuddled up to her chest, and he was so peaceful she was reluctant to stir and put him in his crib.

While sitting there holding Tommy and gently rocking, she thought about her life now that she was alone. She saw herself going back to decorating and designing buildings. She thought of the Loft apartments and their success. They had planned another real estate project, but that wouldn't happen now. Or would it? Why couldn't she carry on? Her latest project, the pavilion, was successful. Her mind wandered, and she had a vision of herself wearing a construction helmet and shaking hands with Mayor Daley. She had just broken ground for a high-rise office building. Photographers crowded around clamoring for pictures. They were eager to give her the praise she so richly deserved as Chicago's first female architect to leave a lasting imprint on Chicago's skyline.

I'll contact our real estate agent as soon as we get back in Chicago. I'll start working on a design, and the building will be called Burnham Towers. It will be a lasting tribute to Jeff, and it will be dedicated to Tommy. She wanted him to be a part of his father's legacy and to share his love for Chicago.

The next morning when she went to get Tommy, he was smiling and waving his arms in the air eager to begin another day. Through his smile, she noticed that two bottom front baby teeth had come through during the night. The timing was perfect. Now he wouldn't be a cranky baby during the car trip home.

*****

Chapter Twenty-Three

At 79, Tom was a handsome, youthful-looking man who had been physically active all his life. Jennie was still attractive, and all during their 45 years of marriage he had always kept the romance fresh between them. He told her frequently that she was the most beautiful woman he'd ever seen. Everyone thought they were the perfect family, and life had been good to them. He had been there when their son and daughter were born; theirs was a solid marriage. The two of them could have been the couple in an ad for healthy, attractive, middle-aged people.

Tom looked forward to their family gatherings on Thanksgiving and Christmas. As usual, they would have Thanksgiving at their home, and they would be going to the Cape for Christmas. It had become a family tradition.

When Jennie woke during the night and Tom wasn't beside her, she thought he was in the bathroom. She waited to hear the flush of the toilet, but the house was eerily silent. *Where can he be,* she thought as she got up and went to the bathroom.

"Oh my God," She uttered. His body was slumped on the floor in front of the sink. A bottle of aspirin was spilled in the sink. She knelt and tried to find a pulse, but there was none. She ran to the phone and dialed 9ll. The operator asked his age and if he had a heart history. The paramedics arrived with a defibrillator. They listened to his heart, checked his pulse, and put the defibrillator on his chest. They put an oxygen mask on him, and Jennie watched in horror as his whole body convulsed when they used the defibrillator again. Then they put him on a gurney and ran for the ambulance. Jennie grabbed her robe and followed them. They took him to Coronary ICU and continued to work on him, but it was useless. The cardiologist told her he had been gone too long to recover. He questioned her, but she told him she didn't know how long he had been in the bathroom before she woke. No, he hadn't complained of chest pains, and she told him about his heart history, and his stents. No, there was nothing unusual about his behavior. They had a late dinner, discussed their upcoming Thanksgiving gathering, watched the news on TV, and went to bed early.

The cardiologist assumed that whenever it started the attack hit him hard, and he died instantly.

Jennie cried and said, "I need him, I can't live without him."

Tom had pre-registered to be a body donor so his body was hurriedly wheeled away, and after the recovery was completed, Jennie would receive his cremated remains.

Jennie called Peggy then went back to the desk in the ICU to complete the necessary forms.

Peggy entered the ICU office carrying Tommy and crying. She couldn't believe that she had talked to her father yesterday, and today he was gone. They clung to each other crying. The shock of seeing him lying on the bathroom floor, gray and lifeless played over and over in Jennie's mind. She took Tommy into her arms, and they walked blindly through the hospital and went home.

She called Charlie, and he couldn't believe what had just happened. He said they would leave immediately. It was nearly nine o'clock on Saturday morning.

Next she called Suz and Matt, and they cried in disbelief. They loved him, why did this have to happen!

Jennie moved quietly around her kitchen making coffee and toast. They weren't hungry, but eating was something to do to pass time. They sat and made a list of everyone who would need to be notified. They would have to wait until his cremated remains were received before they could have a memorial service. Peggy didn't know that her father had willed his body to science; it was never mentioned. Jennie would have his ashes sent to the mortuary. They would have the service at the Presbyterian Church they had attended for 45 years. His ashes would be buried in a nearby cemetery, and her ashes in time would be buried next to his. She would get one marker with both names inscribed on it. So many arrangements had to be made in a short time.

The following day, Charlie, Lisa and Sara arrived, and the crying began again. Charlie was upset and commented that they were completely unprepared – "usually there's an illness or other forewarning." He told Jennie he had never in his entire life felt as lonely as when he got the news.

Soon condolences were pouring in from Northwestern and the Kellogg School of Business, Speaker's Platform and the organizations where he had lectured, his publisher, McGraw-Hill, and countless friends and acquaintances.

Tom's funeral was held on Wednesday afternoon. Jennie sat in the front pew with her children, her daughter-in-law, and Suz and Matt. The church was filled with people who knew both of them. Jennie looked pale and grief-stricken as she entered on the arm of her son.

The service was brief and touching, and after the ceremony they along with close friends went to Tony's for coffee and dessert. Jennie felt it was fitting to be together at the place where she met Tom and where they went often.

She said to Matt, "What am I going to do now?"

"I think you get through it day by day," he said, "that's all you can do. And one day you'll feel better. It'll never be the same, but you go on. You have your kids and your friends. People mend and survive it."

"Maybe I should sell the house on the Cape."

"It's too soon to make that decision. Don't do anything yet," he replied.

Matt and Suz sat with her for a long time, not talking, just being together. Their closeness meant more to her than words.

*****

Jennie looked as though she was in a trance as she went from room to room hoping the past week had been a bad dream and somehow Tom would still be alive. She looked at his closet and closed the door; *it's too soon, I can't do this now, but when? Will it be easier next week? How can I live here without him?* She had never felt so lonely in her life. Forty-five wonderful years of marriage had ended in a single instant.

She went into the bathroom and noticed a pair of jeans hanging on the hook at the back of the door. They were old jeans, faded at the knees. He had worn them the day that he died. She pressed the jeans to her face hoping for a scent of him. She took them off the hook and heard change in the pockets and the crinkle of papers. She reached into a back pocket and found a wad of papers and a fold of money, several ones and a twenty. There was a receipt from the hardware store for an extension cord and a package of light bulbs. Another receipt from Neiman-Marcus for a robe. Oh, my Christmas present, she thought. There was also a dry cleaning receipt and two lottery tickets. She didn't know that Tom played the lottery.

The phone rang. It was Suz, "Can you join me for lunch?"

"Oh, Suz," It's so nice of you, but I'm not hungry. I'm trying to sort through Tom's things, but I don't know where to start."

"You don't have to make those decisions now. I'll bring some soup and sandwiches, and we'll think about it together. You have to eat and stay strong, your children need you."

When Suz arrived carrying a shopping bag, she went to the kitchen and heated the chicken soup and made sandwiches. Jennie began eating the soup, but refused the sandwich.

Suz reminded her that Thanksgiving was two weeks away asking, "You are going to have your usual gathering, aren't you? Charlie and Peggy will expect it, it's a family tradition. They are suffering too. You all need each other more than ever now."

You are right, Suz. It'll be up to me to keep the family together."

*****

Jennie worried about Peggy having lost her beloved husband and now her father, but she seemed to be making a complete turnaround. She threw herself into her work with a vengeance, and Tommy was her only diversion.

She found a vacant lot in Streeterville that would be ideal for an office building, and she decided to collaborate with another architect for the initial work. He had been a friend of Jeff's and his name was Todd Martin. He was a partner in an up-and-coming architectural firm in Chicago. Streeterville had suddenly become the hot location for development because it was the only place where there were vacant sites near Lake Michigan and the Chicago River. However, the residents were not happy with the news that a 28-story high-rise office building would be built on the site. They were afraid their neighborhood would end up like Manhattan, resulting in high-rise canyons towering over gridlocked traffic. Also, they envisioned parking problems. Peggy tried to allay their fears by pointing out that with the addition of her office building, they would be able to live and work in Streeterville; they would no longer have to commute elsewhere for employment.

As a concession, she altered her plans to include an underground parking garage for 200 vehicles. Then they received approval from the ward alderman whose approval was required. Aldermen were still powerful in Chicago politics.

Todd forewarned her that Chicago traditions were changing, and contemporary architecture was replacing bland buildings made of concrete and brick. "Streeterville is a glitzy new community; and glass and steel would fit in well," he told her.

She had hired Todd to do preliminary work such as a feasibility study and site analysis. Also, she was aware that he was well known in City Hall and had experience in working through the maze of municipal authorities for getting building permits, zoning and other regulations approved. She also wanted his expertise in selecting a General Contractor since he had worked with several in the area. He wondered, *does she just want me to be a grunt and not add anything to the design?* Peggy sensed his feelings, and she didn't want to alienate him so she had to walk a fine line.

But Todd felt sorry for Peggy knowing her lack of experience in designing high-rise buildings so he surreptitiously gave advice even though she didn't ask for it. He would say, "based upon our experience with… or "we spent days researching such and such," when she was faced with finding the most-energy efficient materials to meet environmental regulations.

He wanted her to realize her dream of honoring Jeff by building a high-rise office building, and he wanted it to be her design with her name as the sole architect. Todd and Jeff had been close friends since their college days, and he wanted to see "Burnham Towers" built as a lasting tribute to him as much as Peggy did. Peggy and Todd worked well together; sometimes Todd picked up food from the Deli, and they worked through lunch.

Todd was an easygoing, tall and lean man with a shock of blond hair. His hair seemed to be an obsession as he combed it often, and there was never a hair out of place. He was divorced and had a five-year old son, so he had an instant rapport with Tommy, and Tommy was quick to identify with Todd as a father figure. One day when he stopped by to check with Peggy on a detail, she was on the phone and Tommy was crying. He picked up Tommy and held him close, and Tommy immediately stopped crying. From then on his face lit up at the sight of Todd.

*****

"Are you going to be able to put your work aside long enough to have Thanksgiving dinner with us? Charlie and Lisa will be here, and Beth said she would love to join us. She said she hasn't seen much of you either."

"Yes, Mom, of course, I want to be with you. I've been so busy with the office project. You know how much work I have right now. Sometimes I feel as if I'm slipping backward as I try to go forward. There's so much to think about."

"That's what has me worried – you seem to be your own worst enemy right now – always putting more on your plate than you can possibly handle."

"Tommy is a constant interruption too. He's still cutting teeth, and he doesn't want to be left alone; he wants to be held all the time."

"Maybe you'll have to hire a baby sitter to help you."

"I've thought of that," Peggy replied. "But Todd has been so helpful; he's a godsend."

"What can I bring for dinner?"

"Nothing,"

"It'll be amusing to see how Tommy reacts to Sara," Peggy replied. She started to speak and then hesitated as if unsure of what to say. "Do you think it would be all right to invite Todd for dinner? He mentioned that he didn't have plans."

"Yes, I think that would be nice. You're business partners, and you're both alone. I think he would like that, and we'd get to know him better. No one should be alone on Thanksgiving when there's so much food to share."

Thanksgiving Day was cold but sunny; however no one's thoughts were centered on the weather. Charlie, Lisa and Sara were the first to arrive with Sam bounding alongside. He had endured his first flight as if he was a seasoned traveler. Peggy and Todd looked like any typical young family with Tommy perched on Todd's shoulder. They greeted one another and began talking as if they had never been apart.

Charlie said, I'm going to train for next summer's annual bicycle race from one end of the Cape to the other to honor Dad. He would have loved to be a participant." Lisa and Peggy said they would honor him by taking longer beach walks.

As Jennie sat back and listened to the exchange of banter that was passed back and forth while eating, she thought, *I don't have to be concerned about keeping my family together. No matter where our lives take us, we will continue to be drawn back to the ocean. She thought about the pleasure they have brought to her life, and she felt a sense of peacefulness settling around the table.*

*****

Jennie wondered if she would ever get used to the dull silence around the house. The phone rang, and she welcomed the shrill ring.

Charlie asked, "Mom, will you be able to come to the Cape for Christmas? Peggy wants to come, and she suggested that the two of you drive together. She says Tommy comes with too much baggage to fly."

"I've been thinking about it, Charlie, this house is so quiet, I need a change. I'm sure that Peggy and I can manage the drive.

"That's great, and you won't be pressured by a time schedule," Charlie replied.

"Yes, Charlie, I have to remind myself that I don't have a schedule, that there's no one waiting for me."

Jennie reflected on her role of wife and mother. She created healthy meals, orchestrated memorable parties and family gatherings; she was the perfect nurturer. She even slammed down the phone when she heard Tom's car pull into the driveway, so she would be there to greet him. He was her lover, her confidante, and her best friend. Now she had only herself to think of and momentarily it gave her pleasure. She would spend summers at the Cape, and she thought of walking the beach and wading in the surf. The phone interrupted her thoughts; and she was pleased and surprised that it was George Anderson at **Cape Cod Magazine.**

"How are you doing, Jennie? Ellen and I were hoping that time and family helped you get through your darkest hours. Are you going to continue to work for the magazine?"

"Yes, of course, George, I'll need my writing more than ever. I even have the next deadline posted on the refrigerator. I'm going to the Cape for Christmas, so we could get together then if you wish."

"That's great; I'd like to meet with you on the 27th. I'm glad to hear you are staying on board."

*****

On a frosty December morning, Jennie and Peggy packed up the Land Rover and got an early start. They had good driving weather, and it was late afternoon on the second day when they arrived in Barnstable. It was beginning to get dark, but they could hear the water slamming up on the shore. After feeding Tommy and getting him ready for bed, she was tired, so she left the boxes and luggage unpacked and went to bed.

The brilliant morning sun brightened the whole house, and Tommy woke up early. Peggy rummaged through the boxes for the coffee and baby food, muttering to herself, I should have done this last night. While the coffee was brewing, she bathed and dressed Tommy. He was in a playful mood, and she laughed and played with him.

The phone rang and Jennie said, "I hope I'm not calling too early. I decided that sausage and eggs would taste good. Why don't you and Tommy join me?"

"Mom, I'd love to. I was just going to look for something to eat. We'll be there shortly."

After breakfast, Peggy was anxious to walk the beach and get some fresh air. "Mom, will you watch Tommy while I go for a walk. After the drive I feel as though I've been sitting for days."

"Yes, of course, dear; take your time, Tommy wants to play."

As she walked she marveled that she owned a home on a beach. Her life has turned out to be a different life than she imagined. She never thought she would be living on Cape Cod, but it was what Jeff wanted. In a way, she felt she was now living his life.

The beach was littered with broken shells, fish bones, hundreds of horseshoe crabs, and an occasional dead gull. Everyone is responsible for keeping the beaches clean, but since it was off season and the summer residents had left, the pristine beaches of summer were gone. Aside from the ever-present gulls, the only life was an angry crow jabbing at a reeking pile of kelp and salt grass near the water's edge.

Up ahead she saw a teen-aged boy with a black garbage bag picking up debris, and she stopped to chat with him. He told her that the residents hired him to pick up their beach areas during the summer, and he continued doing it in off season. Peggy told him she would like to have him keep her beach clean, and he told her he charged $10.00 a week.

"You've got a job."

*****

"'Tis the season to be jolly," or so the familiar carol goes, but Jennie wasn't feeling festive. She told herself that it didn't matter if the family was together for Christmas; without Tom, some things would never be the same. Then she thought that Christmas was a time of selflessness and her children and grandchildren deserved their traditional holiday celebration.

She went to the attic to get the Christmas ornaments and artificial tree. She smiled as she grabbed the Twister game that Charlie had given Tom last year. After she had brought the boxes down to the living room, she muttered "bah humbug." *What's wrong with me, I want to decorate the house one minute and not be bothered the next.*

Just then Peggy and Tommy entered the room. "Mom, let's go and get a live tree. The house will smell festive and we'll get into the spirit of Christmas." She put her arm around her mother and said, "We both feel sadness this Christmas. So many things come to mind; neither Jeff nor Dad will see Tommy's first Christmas."

"I know, and it's difficult. Your father and I created rituals for over forty years, never thinking that one day everything would come to a grinding halt."

"I know what you are saying, but it doesn't have to mean an end to family Christmas gatherings."

Jennie smiled and said, "Let's go find a tree."

Since we're having Christmas Eve at my house, we have to shop for food, too. What shall I serve?"

"It will be a late supper after church services, so let's make it easy and pick up lobster bisque from the Lobster Pot like we did last year."

"That sounds good. Let's go to the lighting of the town Christmas tree tonight."

While weaving the lights in and out of their live Christmas tree, Jennie told Peggy that George Anderson at Cape Cod Magazine wanted to see her after Christmas, and she wondered what he had in mind.

"You're going to continue writing your articles, aren't you?"

"Oh yes. I need that outlet more than ever now."

"Maybe he'll give you a different assignment, be a roving reporter or something."

After they finished decorating the tree, they tried the lights and sat back to admire their accomplishment.

"Now it'll really smell like Christmas," Peggy said as she took some fragrant blue juniper branches from a plastic bag and arranged them on the mantel. "With the flickering candles and the wonderful aroma of the greens, it really seems like Christmas now," Jennie said.

On Christmas Eve day Charlie and Lisa arrived with Sara and Sam. Charlie hugged Jennie and asked, "How're you doing, Mom? You look great."

"I'm learning to survive alone. There's never a rehearsal for this."

"In time you'll actually enjoy being alone and being completely independent. You're financially independent, you don't have health problems, and you have your writing to keep you busy."

"You're right, Charlie. I've thought about spending more time here at the Cape; it's easier to be independent here. Like you and Lisa, I've come to love the Cape, and I want to live here. When your father and I bought here, we knew it would be more than a summer home."

"I hope our families will always make the time to return here for Christmas," Lisa said.

"I do too," Peggy chimed in. "It's good to leave the craziness of the city and come here where the only noise is the roar of the ocean. I envy you and Charlie in driving distance, where you can pop in and pop out. After the office building is completed, I'm going to spend a lot more time here."

"I'm happy to hear that, Peggy." Jennie replied. She glanced at her watch and announced that it was time to leave for the 6 p.m. Christmas Eve service.

They walked in silence as they approached the church, and they were surprised to see spot lights outside the church illuminating the double doors that had been festooned with generous green wreaths with red bows. It was a sign that the church was going through better times. They noticed that the aged floor boards had been given a fresh coat of varnish, and the altar area was adorned with red poinsettia plants. The sanctuary had lost some of its frugal Puritan demeanor. The Sunday school class dressed in appropriate costumes portrayed the timeless birth of Jesus, and Sara was spellbound.

After the service they all returned to Peggy's place for a lobster bisque supper and the opening of presents.

As usual, Charlie and Lisa hosted the dinner on Christmas day, this year an elegant beef tenderloin roast with sautéed new potatoes, green beans with toasted almonds and Caesar salad. Charlie prided himself on becoming an accomplished chef. "This year you're really in for a treat."

Lisa had started a large jigsaw puzzle, and she invited everyone to help find the pieces. They would also enjoy Scrabble and games of Rummy.

They reflected on the loss of Jeff and their father, and Charlie stated that in his role of patriarch, he would keep the family together. Let's promise to always be together on Thanksgiving and Christmas.

Chapter Twenty-Four

Jennie drove through Barnstable, past the hardware store, the five and ten cent store, and a new book store; she mentally made a note to return to check it out. She arrived at the office of Cape Cod Magazine and glanced at the dashboard clock. It was 9:05. Her meeting with George Anderson wasn't until 9:30. Since she was early and she hadn't had breakfast, she parked and ran into the coffee shop next door for coffee and a doughnut.

Anderson extended his hand and heartily greeted her saying, "It's good to see you again, Jennie. C'mon in. You look wonderful." She noticed that his shoulders were stooped, and he walked slow as he led her into his office.

"It's good to see you; it's good to be at the Cape, and I'm surprised to see so little snow on the ground," she said. There had been a light dusting during the night, and the sun was not yet out to melt it.

"Yes, this year so far we got off easy. It'll be gone before noon."

His demeanor changed to a serious look, and he moved closer. "Jennie, I wish I could say that everything's fine and dandy, but that would be a lie. I've been having health problems, and I want to retire. Ellen and I want to do all the things we promised to do when I retired. Of course, my biggest concern is the magazine. I don't want it to fail, so I have to find a qualified person to take over my job as editor, and you are that person."

Jennie gasped in surprise, but she let him continue.

"I've been very impressed with your writing and your genuine interest in Cape Cod. Our subscriptions increased considerably since you joined the staff. It's very evident that you care about the Cape, and you want to see our unique way of life continue. That's precisely the image we want to convey to our readers. I realize you are still grieving over the loss of your husband; sometimes the call to a second journey in life commences when unexpected change is thrust upon us. You may find this new journey in your life is just what you needed to help you heal."

He abruptly stopped speaking and waited for Jennie's reply.

"I'm almost speechless. Thank you for all your kind words. What can I say? It's a dream come true. Of course, I'll accept the position, and I do so because I sincerely love the Cape and I can't say enough good things about it. It truly is a unique spot in our country, and I'd like to spend more time here – possibly live here year around."

He rose and reached out his hand to congratulate her. "I'm happy that I didn't have to beg you to take over the magazine."

*****

When Jennie returned home she went to the post office to pick up the mail. Normally, that was Tom's job, but there would be no more dividing of chores. Leafing through the envelopes, she noticed a Neiman-Marcus return address on one envelope. It piqued her interest, and she tore the envelope open to find a delivery receipt for a package to be delivered to 3213 Lakeview Avenue. *That's just six blocks from here.* The receipt didn't contain a name, just the address. Further down on the receipt it stated, "Robe to arrive Dec. 20." She clutched the receipt tightly and leaned against the wall for support. Her knees buckled, and she slid down its length. When she came to she was trembling. She felt like throwing up and went to the bathroom, but nothing came up. She went for a walk, the street crowded with people on their way somewhere. There was purpose in their lives. She felt out of place and returned to her familiar bedroom and cried herself to sleep.

It was three in the morning when she woke, and she needed something to revitalize her. She went to the shower and let the warm water massage her tired muscles. While showering, she thought about her future being at the helm of the magazine and how little time she had to prepare for the move. *I'll put all this behind me; I don't know the full story, and I don't need to know. Tom and I loved each other, and we had a good life. I've been left with beautiful memories, and I'll keep it that way. Charlie and Peggy will never know about this.*

She decided to sell the house in Chicago and live at the Cape year around. She would become a "Codder." She had raised her children and sustained a marriage and now she was ready for adventure. *I've been fitting my personal life and needs around my work ever since "A Brief Wondrous Life became a best seller – on top of which I've had two grandchildren arrive and a husband retire. I never had a chance to recharge. Now I'm going to regenerate myself and live the life I always thought could only exist in a dream.*

The day before Jennie was to leave for the Cape, Suz arranged a get-together with a few friends to bid her a fond farewell. She was led to the living room where votive candles glittered around the room, and the coffee table was laden with every imaginable kind of finger food – artichoke dip, smoked salmon on pumpernickel, mixed nuts, salsa and chips. Suz greeted her asking, "Would you like a glass of red or white?"

"Thank you, Suz, this is great, just what I wanted tonight, the quiet company of good friends and a chance to catch my breath."

"So," Roxanne began, "You're finally taking some time to relax; it's been three months since we've seen you and now you're leaving Chicago for good!"

"Well," Jennie apologetically stated, "I got a fantastic job offer on the Cape…"

Susan interrupted, "When are you going to slow down, smell the roses, so to speak? You've written nine books, raised a family, and traveled with your husband from one coast to the other on countless speaking engagements. When are you going to take time for yourself?"

"You girls don't understand. I like what I do. You used to hold high-pressure jobs before retiring; you should be more sympathetic. Not everyone has the opportunity to become the editor of a major magazine. I'm excited, and I'm going to give it all I've got. But I'm looking forward to some adventure, too."

"Does adventure mean a new man in your life?" Suz asked.

Everyone laughed. "Well for starters," Jennie replied, "I was thinking of getting my hair streaked, buying a sexy new bathing suit, and hiking the beach. In that order. Seriously, I want all of you to come visit me. I have a big old house right on the beach. We could have lots of fun."

She left the party with a feeling of excitement, that she was beginning a new life.

But leaving the duplex that they had lovingly restored to a one-owner home wasn't easy, and she wondered if she would regret it later. Those thoughts ran through her mind as she crammed the last bag into her already cramped trunk and slammed down the lid.

She leaned her forehead on the roof of the car and began to cry. Her friends had said she was brave to go off on her own, that they wished they had the guts to do the same. She raised her chin and placed a finger under her nose to keep more tears from flowing. She looked back at the house and thought, *if I linger, I might change my mind.*

She climbed in the car and didn't look back. The light turned red, and she came to a stop. She thought of her new job as editor, what it entailed, her leadership responsibility, meetings with staff and non-staff, and lunches that were no longer social. The light turned green, and she stepped on the gas. *Everything will be fine.*

*****

The City of Barnstable notified Peggy that the Jeffrey Burnham Pavilion had been completed, and they wanted to have the dedication ceremony on Memorial Day, which was the opening of the concert season, and it would also be an appropriate occasion to commemorate Jeff. Peggy was in complete agreement, and she began to make plans for the trip to the Cape. It would be a family affair.

Everything fell into place – the design of the office building was complete and construction would begin. She and Todd met with the construction foreman to finalize details so she would be free to leave. Todd wanted to be there for the dedication so he would drive with Peggy and Tommy, then fly back to Chicago. Beth opted to fly in and out of Boston, and Jennie would meet her flight. Peggy would stay at the Cape for the summer, and Todd would oversee the construction of Burnham Tower.

Despite the frantic pace of traveling and the solemenness of the occasion, the party atmosphere of vacationers returning to the Cape for a summer of fun was transmitted to Peggy. She was cheerful and energetic as she went about the duties of surviving widow.

The sky and the ocean were the same shade of blue, with whitecaps gently rolling in to the shore. Flags were unfurled at every conceivable location up and down the Cape. It would be a perfect Memorial Day. Tommy awoke at the first hint of daylight, and Peggy wasn't dismayed. This was going to be an extraordinary day, and she didn't want to waste any of it by lolling in bed.

After the dedication ceremony and the concert, they would all gather at Jennie's big house with the blue shutters for a family reunion and barbeque. Charlie and Lisa along with the rest of the family would wander in and out to the beach, the first of many summer get-togethers. They would all take their towels and umbrellas to the beach to stake out their place in the sun.

A large crowd of people from all over the Cape gathered around the new pavilion to see and hear the U.S. Marine band. They had heard about the pavilion's high-tech sound system that was amplified through twenty-four speaker towers connected to the stage by radio. Some said the sound would be heard as far away as Provincetown!

In his speech, William Walsh, the mayor of Barnstable said, "This afternoon we are here to dedicate this pavilion and honor the memory of Jeffrey Burnham. After Jeffrey Burnham was tragically lost at sea as a result of a surfing accident, his wife, Peggy, designed this music pavilion to honor the memory of her beloved husband, and to give back to the community they cherished. Mrs. Burnham gave a generous donation of $3 million to the City of Barnstable to have the pavilion built for the enjoyment of the entire community and music lovers from near and far."

Peggy, leading Tommy by his hand, moved up to the microphone. "Thank you, Mr. Walsh, and all of you for attending this dedication. My husband loved the Cape, the ocean, and all that the Cape and its way of life embodied. Jeff often said he would like to spend the rest of his life here, and, in a way, his wish has been fulfilled. Our son, Tommy, who didn't have the opportunity to know his father, will be able to look at this pavilion and see a lasting memorial to his father."

"Please sit back and enjoy the beautiful music of our United States Marine band. Again, thank you all for coming. Have a happy Memorial Day."

The crowd gave her a thunderous round of applause. Todd's pride was evident as he stood and hugged her when she returned to her seat.

*****

Jennie thought as she was hanging a picture, this is the first time I've had an office away from home where my time will be better respected, and she recalled the countless interruptions of her children.

Charlie barging in and saying, "Mom, where's my red shirt?"

Peggy crying and needing a hug and a band aid when she fell and scraped a knee.

As she gazed out the window behind her desk, she could see the harbor and the long piers and docks, the whale-watching boats, majestic sails, shops and restaurants.

She heard a light knock on the partially-opened office door, and she swung her chair around to see who was intruding on her daydreaming.

"Sorry to startle you," he said as his face broke into an easy smile. "I'm Ed Stern, and I head up the Barnstable Chamber of Commerce." He was a lanky, gentle-looking man with salt and pepper hair, who seemed to personify a life of second chances. With his permanently tanned face, he had the look of a man who loved the sea and boating.

"I wanted to stop by to meet you. We rely on your magazine for advertising and feature articles, so we'll be spending a lot of time together," he said.

"Oh, it's nice to meet you, I'm Jennie Doyle, the new editor."

"Yes, I know, George told me all about you, well not all, he told me a lot about you."

"Then I need to know more about you."

"I just closed the office for the day, and I thought I'd take the boat out. It's down there in the harbor, and he pointed toward the docks. Come with me, and I'll tell you about the Chamber and what I do."

Jennie's cheeks burned with delight when she saw a beautiful yacht in the harbor, and they were walking toward it. She couldn't believe that she was going sailing in a yacht with a complete stranger. She looked around at the other boats also getting ready to go out to sea, and noted a grin on the face of the man in the boat next to Ed's. Ed waved to him, and she wondered if her presence would be the start of small town gossip.

He put the key into the ignition, the motor started, and the boat glided out of the harbor. Jennie's heart was racing as she stood next to him at the wheel behind the windshield. He cranked the engine, and she felt the increase in speed. They were flying over the surface of the water, bucking the waves, and a thrill of excitement ran through her. She had acted on impulse, and the adventure was exhilarating. Then he cut the engine and dropped the anchor. She watched him work as he moved about the deck.

"There we go," he said turning back to her. He led her down the steps to the cabin below. It was like a plush living room all built into the boat. He went to the small refrigerator and took out a bottle of wine and some cheese, and then grabbed two glasses and a box of crackers from a cupboard.

When they were seated with their glasses in hand, he said, "Now we can relax and talk. I like to come here at the end of the day to unwind."

"This is the perfect place to unwind, you have a beautiful boat."

"My wife and I bought it with the thought of cruising up and down the coast, but she didn't get to see that happen. Cancer. Pancreatic cancer, the worst kind."

"I'm sorry to hear that. My husband died instantly, heart attack. What was it like for you? Sometimes I think the survivor, the person left behind, suffers the most."

"It was difficult at first, the loneliness, the feeling of life being meaningless, but I became engrossed in my work, and, realizing that I had a life to live, the task of reinventing my life. That's enough about me, let's talk about you. I understand that in addition to writing for the magazine, you're a published author."

"Yes, I've had nine books published so far."

"So far? You have another book in the back of your mind?"

"It depends upon what happens to me as an editor, how much time I'll have."

They talked about their jobs and their children. His two grown sons live in opposite ends of the country and only get home for Christmas.

"It seems I've been saying good-bye to my boys ever since they left college and home. But it wasn't always that way. Before they were married they came home fairly often."

"My children have made a pact that regardless of what happens in our lives, we will always be together for Thanksgiving and Christmas. Our family has always been together on those holidays, and its comforting to know we can always look forward to those unceremonious events," Jennie replied.

Soon the sun was setting over the water, and Ed said, "I know a place with great food and music where we could have dinner."

"Sounds wonderful."

They were flying over the surface of the water, and the sounds of the wind and the engine made talk impossible. She admired his strong hands as they gripped the steering wheel and effortlessly steered the boat into its slip.

*****

The next morning Jennie called Suzanne. "Suz, I've met the most wonderful man."

"So soon?"

"Yes, and it immediately felt like we were old friends reuniting old ties of friendship. Haven't you ever met someone that you simply liked as a good friend?"

"Yes, we were twenty years old, and his hormones were raging. Seriously, there's nothing wrong with a second marriage at this stage in your life. You have many productive years ahead of you, and you should spend them with someone you like and enjoy being with."

"It's too premature to even think of marriage. For the time being, I'll settle for a good conversationalist. This big old house gets very quiet."

"Before I forget, tell Charlie that old Mrs. Dillard died; she was over 100 years old," Suz said.

"He will be sad to hear that. He liked her a lot. She looked worn and tired the last time we saw her," Jennie replied.

"Let's stay in touch, Suz, and I'll let you know what happens with my new friend."

Almost overnight the thrill of the challenge became a new life for Jennie. She spent long hours in her office, talking on the phone, answering letters, meeting with staff, reading and editing the material for each issue, and writing her own comments for the editorial page.

One humid August Saturday morning Jennie was relaxing on the porch, coffee cup in hand, when Charlie bicycled up the driveway. "So you finally made it to the porch – first time in three months."

"What are you talking about?" she asked.

"Mother, the only time you have left the office in months is on Sundays, and then you always seemed distracted. It's time that you spent more time outside."

"Charlie, you know how much work I've had just starting a new job. But things are getting to be more routine now. I talked to Suz a week ago, and she told me to tell you that Mrs. Dillard died. She was over 100 years old."

"I'm sorry to hear that; I liked her a lot. When I totaled the Gremlin, she commiserated with me instead of reprimanding me. She turned 100 on Christmas Day. I gave Dad some money and told him to get something nice for her. She sent me a thank you note and told me she liked the pretty robe. But I came here to tell you we're having a farewell barbeque tonight. I have to leave early to get back to school. Columbia is starting everything earlier this year; we used to wait until after Labor Day. Peggy and Tommy will be there, and it would be nice to have Ed join us."

"Of course, I'll be there, Charlie, and I'll see if Ed is free," as she stood to go inside.

As soon as she crossed the threshold, tears came, and she cried as if the tears had been held back for ages. As she sobbed, she softly cried out, "I'm so sorry, Tom."

She heard the crunch of tires on the gravel driveway, and went to the window expecting to see the mailman or the meter reader. Ed opened the screen door before she could get to it. He gave her a hug and kissed her wet cheek.

"You've been crying, Jennie, what happened?"

She led him to the sofa, and tears trickled down her cheeks as she told him about the robe and her feelings of guilt and remorse for suspecting that Tom was having an affair.

Ed kissed her and told her it was okay to cry.

She felt his quiet strength and reveled in his simple kindness. "I don't know whether I'm crying from guilt or relief to learn that there wasn't an affair. I'll be okay now; I'm sorry you had to see me this way."

"I'll kiss away your tears whenever you are sad. Where would you like to have dinner tonight?"

"We're invited to Charlie and Lisa's tonight. They're having a farewell to summer barbeque. Charlie has to leave early to go back to school. Is that okay?"

"Yes, that's great. I like being with your family."

"Well that's good to hear, they like you a lot."

"It's a beautiful afternoon; let's go for a walk on the beach. Charlie is right; you've been working too hard."

"I did put in some long hours at first, but now that my first issue has been published, I've relaxed considerably."

"And that issue was every bit as good as anything George put out. It's evident that you love the Cape and its way of life."

"Yes, I do love the Cape and have always thought about living here year around, although I wasn't supposed to be living here alone."

"I'm glad you made the decision to move here." He put his arm around her and kissed her in full view of the two old fishermen lounging on the marina bench.

Jennie and Ed and Lisa and Charlie were relaxing on the porch with a glass of wine while Sara played with Sam on the beach. The night air was balmy and not too humid; they wanted to watch the sun set over the ocean. A seagull strutted near the water's edge searching for food. Sam took off after it, and it swooped into the sky. Of course, Sara ran after Sam. Charlie picked up a beach ball and headed for the beach to keep her away from the surf. He loved the beach and he wasn't happy about having to go back to the city before Labor Day. Lisa slipped from her perch on the porch rail and went inside for a tray of cheese and crackers.

Later, Peggy made an abrupt entrance exclaiming, "Todd called and said the ironworkers will be topping off next week. Then the site will be swarming with framers, electricians, and other trades people. The leasing agent said it is 75% leased. I'm going to close the house and go back to Chicago; I want to be there for the topping off celebration."

"You'll be here alone, Mom. Will that be okay?"

Ed reached over and placed his hand on hers.

"Everything will be fine, Charlie."